My So-Called Afterlife

Tamsyn Murray was born in Cornwall in the Chinese Year of the Rat. This makes her charming, creative and curious (on a good day) but also selfish, restless and impatient (v. v. bad day).

After moving around a lot during her early years, she now lives in London with her husband and her daughter. At least her body does. Her mind tends to prefer imaginary places and wanders off whenever it can but that's not necessarily a bad thing in a writer.

When she isn't making things up, you might find Tamsyn on the stage, pretending to be someone else. She occasionally auditions for TV talent shows. One day she might get past the first round . . .

Find out more about Tamsyn at her website:
www.tamsynmurray.co.uk

My So-Called Afterlife

TAMSYN MURRAY

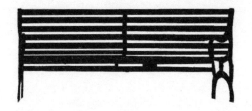

PICCADILLY PRESS · LONDON

To Lee, for providing the snugs and making sure I ate. (IDDY)
To Tania, for putting up with the endless demands to
'Just read this'. (And yeah, you're right. You are my muse.)

First published in Great Britain in 2010
by Piccadilly Press Ltd,
5 Castle Road, London NW1 8PR
www.piccadillypress.co.uk

A catalogue record for this book is available
from the British Library

ISBN: 978 1 84812 057 0 (paperback)

3 5 7 9 10 8 6 4

Printed and bound by CPI Group (UK) Ltd, Croydon, CR0 4YY
Cover design by Patrick Knowles

Chapter 1

I knew it was time to move on when a tramp peed on my Uggs.

OK, he didn't do it on purpose – it may even have been my fault for not looking where I was going – but it was still the single most disgusting thing to happen to me that week.

'Eeeuw! Gross!' I let out a howl of dismay and stepped backwards through the urinal. 'Do you have any idea how much these cost?'

Utterly unconcerned, the tramp finished his business and headed for the stairs. Sourly, I watched him leave. 'Next time, wee on your own feet,' I called after him. Although, judging from the trail of soggy footprints, he already had. And, like pretty much all my visitors, he didn't stop to wash his hands. I suppose he had an excuse. If you smell like the inside of a rubbish bin, hygiene probably isn't your top priority.

It wasn't the first time I'd found myself ankle-deep in wee. When you haunt a public toilet, an over-familiarity with the more basic human functions goes with the territory. In the early days, I often found myself sinking into the floor or through whatever I happened to be sitting on, but it didn't take me long to adjust to having less substance than candyfloss. Once the novelty of walking through walls and defying gravity had worn off, I spent most of my time hiding in the cleaners' stock cupboard, with its shelves of loo roll and fascinating bottles of cleaning fluid, bored out of my mind. The difference that day was Jeremy – he'd given me hope that I wasn't destined to hang around the men's toilets on the corner of Carnaby Street for the rest of my days.

You've probably guessed by now that I'm not your average fifteen-year-old girl. Before my death I was pretty normal. My favourite part of myself was my hair – dark and silky, it looked awesome when I bothered to straighten it. Freya, my best mate and partner in crime, used to go on about my eyes, which she described as 'exotically emerald'. I lost count of the times we found ourselves in detention for slathering on forbidden eyeliner and mascara. The target of our efforts was the gorgeous Jamie Bickerstaffe. Accept no substitutes, Jamie was the official babe-magnet of St Augustine's Secondary. I had been determined that one day he'd know who I was, and I guess eventually he did. Just not in the way that I'd hoped.

Apart from the pointless rules and casual bullying,

school was mostly bearable. I wasn't the coolest kid, but I wasn't a geek either. To this day, I thank my lucky stars I didn't die in school uniform, or I'd have been stuck in a poo-coloured blazer for all eternity. Who knows, there may be a God after all.

Jeremy was no different to anyone else the evening he first walked in. I was going through a phase of grading my visitors according to their toilet habits. You wouldn't believe what some people do when they're alone in the loo. Then again, maybe you would.

He was a hummer. In fact, it was his tuneless rendition of the Jackson Five's 'Blame it on the Boogie' that tempted me out of my cupboard to give him the once over.

Critically, I studied his battered biker jacket and grey jeans. From behind, he looked like a geography teacher trying to be down with the kids. That lost him points. He made up for it with his musical taste, though. As my dad always said, anyone who was a fan of early Michael Jackson couldn't be all bad.

His image in the mirror showed me he wasn't as ancient as I'd imagined at first. In spite of his thinning blond hair, I guessed he was in his mid-twenties. Overall, he wasn't scoring badly on the disdain-ometer. In fact, if he didn't fart and washed his hands, he was in with a shot at the top ten most pleasant guests that week.

And then everything changed. He looked up.

'Aaaargh!'

Stumbling backwards, he tugged at his zip, face flooding

with horrified embarrassment. 'How long have you been there?'

I resisted the temptation to glance behind me. 'Are you talking to me?'

'Who else is here?' Turning, he glared at me. 'This is the *men's* toilets. You should be in the ladies' next door.'

My mind fizzed furiously. He could see me. He could actually *see* me! I could have hugged him. Well, I couldn't, but you know what I mean.

'Let me get this straight. You can see and hear me?'

His expression changed. He was starting to look like he regretted engaging me in conversation.

'Are you here on your own?' he said with an exaggerated slowness, like I was four years old. That put my back up.

I rolled my eyes. 'Nah, I'm here with my mates for an illegal rave. Of course I'm on my own.'

He smiled, in what I suppose he thought was a reassuring way. It made him look like a deranged kids' TV presenter. 'Right, I'm going to find some help. You stay here.'

Without taking his eyes off me, he crossed to the bottom of the stairs. Almost as an afterthought, he stopped to rinse his hands under the tap. I watched him go with a mixture of curiosity and irritation. Six months I'd been dead and, despite some heavy duty arm-waving and shouting, no one had ever seen me before. It was just my luck that the one person who had was drippier than the log flume at Alton Towers.

Five minutes later he was back, with a member of

London's finest in tow. I groaned. Before I died, I'd held the police in reasonably high esteem. I'd seen them on TV. They spent their days chasing criminals and didn't rest until they had their man. The complete dog's dinner they'd made of the investigation into my death had changed my views. These days, I couldn't shake the impression that most of them would struggle to find their arse with both hands.

'There she is, officer.'

The policeman peered around the apparently empty room. A smile tugged at my lips; this was going to be more entertaining than I'd thought.

'Where?'

Jeremy threw him a hard look and pointed directly at me. 'There.'

Following the line of his finger, the policeman frowned. 'I don't see anyone.'

'She's right in front of you!' Jeremy said, annoyance beginning to creep into his voice. 'Standing by the sinks and making a very rude gesture, I might add.'

With a suspicious sideways look, the policeman said, 'Have you been drinking, sir?'

'No, I flipping well haven't,' Jeremy exploded. 'I came down here to use the facilities and found this . . . this . . . Peeping Tomasina watching me. Between you and me, I don't think she's all there.'

'Hello?' I waved a sarcastic hand. 'I can hear you, you moron. I'm dead, not deaf.'

Jeremy frowned, as though he didn't quite believe what

he'd heard. 'Are you going to do anything about her or not?'

PC Plod pulled himself up to his full height. 'Don't take that tone with me, sir. There's no one in this room besides us, and if anyone's a few spanners short of a socket set, it's you.' His bushy eyebrows beetled together forbiddingly. 'You do realise that wasting police time is a criminal offence?'

'I'm sorry I started this.' Jeremy crossed his arms and sighed. 'Let's cut to the chase. You cannot see or hear a teenage girl doing a terrible monkey impression in front of you right this minute?'

The policeman didn't even look. 'No, sir.'

Jeremy stared first at him, then at me. 'Fine. I haven't been drinking, but maybe I should. In fact, I'm going to start now.'

He turned and stomped his way across the tiled floor.

'Bye!' I called sweetly, wiggling my fingers at his retreating back. 'Do drop in again!'

His shoulders stiffened as he went up the stairs and then he was gone. Shaking his head, the police officer followed, leaving me alone. My grin slowly evaporated. The bloke might have been a prize plonker, but at least he'd known I was there. Now I was on my own again. A lump began to form in my throat. Maybe the chimp impression had been a mistake.

Chapter 2

The loneliness hit me almost before their footsteps had died away. Over the previous months I'd grown used to being ignored, walked through and occasionally weed on and, apart from the peeing, I'd learned to put up with it all. I took a small crumb of comfort from the fact that I'd been seen at all. Hopefully, there were others who would liven up my dull existence. A gorgeous Hollywood A-lister would be good. Or the lead singer of TNT, who had the entire female population fainting with lust. He'd do.

After twenty minutes of trying to kid myself I wasn't watching the stairs, I went back to my cupboard and stared at the mop bucket. It didn't smell fresh, probably because the cleaners never gave the mop more than a quick rinse before stuffing it into the bucket and locking the door at the end of their shift. The pong brought back memories of school; Simon Henderson smelled exactly like this. Had his parents been toilet attendants? Automatically, my brain skittered away from the thought. I was in danger of breaking my Number One Rule: Never Think About My Old Existence. In the early days, the ache for my friends and family had torn me up inside, but I'd quickly learned that thinking of them only led to agonising tears, and blubbing made my ghostly face go just as blotchy as it had when I was alive. I'd been surprised at first that ghostly status didn't make you transparent – I looked every bit as real as I'd always done. To me, anyway.

'Hello?'

The voice echoed around the deserted cubicles. I didn't move. A few months ago I'd investigated a similar call and had been faced with one middle-aged man passionately embracing another. I spent the next quarter of an hour with my fingers jammed firmly in my ears and my eyes shut, singing at the top of my voice. It brought a whole new meaning to coming out of the closet.

'I know you're here, Teenage Monkey Girl.'

I straightened and poked my head through the door. It was him: Mr Trying-Too-Hard Geography Teacher.

'What do you want?'

The sight of my disembodied head hovering in mid-air clearly shocked him because the colour drained from his face. 'Oh God, I'm hallucinating.'

Rolling my eyes, I rose and stepped into the brightly lit room. 'Don't be such a drama queen. What's the matter –

never seen a ghost before?'

His mouth hung open for a few more seconds before he made a supreme effort to get himself together. 'A g-ghost?' His voice shook as he passed a hand across his drawn face. 'No, strangely enough. Maybe I shouldn't have had that last pint.'

'I don't know why you can see me either, but I don't think you can blame the fact that you've had a skinful.'

Even in his terrified state, he was automatically on the defensive. 'I'm not drunk. I may be losing my mind and scared witless, but I'm hardly steaming. Anyway, you don't look like a ghost. Aren't you supposed to be see-through?'

My patience was wearing thinner than a pole-dancer's thong. 'Look, take my word for it. I really am a ghost. Now either deal with it or go away.'

He eyed me doubtfully. Raising his chin, he reached up and squeezed a section of his cheek between his fingers. 'I expect I'll wake up in a minute.'

'You can pinch yourself as much as you like. It won't make me disappear.' I waved my arms over my head and floated a metre or so off the ground, a trick I'd only recently got the hang of. Gravity still rules supreme, even for ghosts. 'Does this help you believe in me? Woo-ooh!'

To his credit, he didn't run screaming for the door. It appeared to be a definite option, though.

I took pity on him. If the situation had been reversed I'd have been out of there at the first sign of weirdness. He deserved some credit for sticking around.

'Honestly, I don't bite,' I offered, trying to sound

friendly. Perhaps a bit of humour would lighten things up. 'The worst I can do is diss your terrible dress sense. Are you wearing that jacket for a bet? You look like a Hell's Angel who does charity work in his spare time.'

He stared at me, white-faced, for several long seconds before his struggling brain seemed to give up the fight and accept what his eyes and ears were telling it. Whatever else I might have been, I wasn't a threat to him. His breath gushed out with a loud whoosh.

'Excellent. My first ghostly encounter and I get a comedian.' With a dubious shake of his head, he stuck out a trembling hand. 'I can't quite believe I'm saying this, but why don't we start again? My name is Jeremy.'

Reminding myself that this was the first human contact I'd had in ages, I toned down my natural sarcasm. 'I'm Lucy. Shaking hands isn't big in the spirit world, by the way.'

Still looking like he was hoping I was part of a really bad dream, he nodded and let his arm fall back to his side. An uncomfortable silence stretched between us.

'So,' he said eventually. 'At the risk of sounding like an idiot, what are you doing here? The men's toilet is hardly a suitable place to – er – hang out.'

Note to self: do not swear. Conversation was great, but why did he have to be such a moron?

'Duh. I haven't got a lot of choice. This is where I was killed. I can't leave. Believe me, I've tried. It's like there's an invisible force-field at the top of the stairs.'

Jeremy went still. 'You were murdered?' His eyes softened

10

as he realised what that meant. 'You must be the girl who was stabbed down here on New Year's Eve.'

Give the man a banana. 'Yep.'

He eyed me wordlessly. It didn't matter. I could practically hear what he was thinking.

'Yes, it was horrible. No, I don't know who my killer was. Yes, it totally sucks haunting a toilet and no, I didn't look at your willy when you were peeing earlier.'

Jeremy puffed out his cheeks and blinked. 'Well, that's the basics covered then.' A tentative smile crept over his face. 'Thanks for not looking.'

I wrinkled my nose. 'No problem. Boy bits are disgusting, anyway.'

He laughed. It was a pleasant sound and one I hadn't heard for a while, if I didn't count the madman who popped in every few days and cackled away to himself in the end cubicle while stuffing packets of biscuits down the toilet.

'Can I do anything to help? It must be boring, being stuck down here.'

My impassioned groan echoed off walls. 'You have no idea. Do you know there are exactly four thousand, three hundred and twenty-seven tiles in here? Or that it takes a vandal three-and-a-half toilet rolls to completely block a toilet?' I thrust my hand into my pocket and hauled out my phone. 'Or that a ghostly mobile is about as much use as a jelly space-hopper.'

One eyebrow raised, he looked interested. 'Can you get a signal?'

A loud tut escaped me. 'No. Who would I be texting, anyway? I don't know any other ghosts.'

'Good point,' he agreed. 'So how can I help?'

'Tell me what's happening in the world. Have I missed anything?'

He ran a hand through his hair. 'Well, let's see. The Prime Minister resigned and his main rival took over. No one expects him to last more than a few months, though, and it could mean a general election.'

Shaking my head, I said, 'Boring. Haven't you got any news worth hearing? What's the latest with the WAGs? How's life in Albert Square? Ooh, has Declan found out about his mum and his best mate yet?'

Jeremy looked blank. 'WAGs? Do you mean *Crufts*?'

I sighed heavily. 'Of all the people in London, the only person who can see me knows nothing.'

'That's not true,' Jeremy objected. 'I know a lot of things.'

'*Interesting*, I was about to add. Knows nothing interesting. Don't you even have a paper I can read?'

He shook his head, then brightened. 'Hang on, though. I know where I can get one.'

Minutes later he was back, free newspaper in hand.

An ungrateful pout snuck over my face. 'It's hardly *Glamour*.'

'It's all I could get. Here you go.' He thrust the paper towards me. It fell to the floor with a pathetic splat.

I glared at him. 'Ha ha. I'm a ghost. We're not great at holding material things.'

'Oh.' Deflated, he gazed at the fallen paper. 'I could open it for you? Turn the pages?'

It was the first useful suggestion he'd made. 'OK, spread it out on the floor and I'll sit down to read it.'

We both looked at the grubby tiles. Even in my formless state, I didn't fancy sitting in a puddle of wee, and hovering above it was too much like hard work.

'How about if I lay it across one of the sinks?'

And that was how it began. As unlikely as it seemed, Jeremy and I hit it off and he agreed to come back. More importantly, he swore he'd bring better news and – fan-flipping-tastic – a TV magazine so I could catch up on the soaps. I discovered Jeremy was twenty-seven, lived in Notting Hill and wasn't a geography teacher. He worked as a lighting engineer in one of the West End theatres, which I had to admit sounded like a pretty cool job. I had mixed feelings about him, though. His presence made my existence almost bearable and at least I had someone to talk to, but I couldn't help wishing he was ten years younger. Still, he made things a thousand times better than they had been. OK, I was still dead and stuck in a place which smelled like a sewer, but not being acquainted with a body snatcher and a mad scientist, there wasn't a lot I could do to change that.

That's pretty much where you came in. Once or twice a week, Jeremy stopped by for an hour or so after his evening shift finished, and I found myself sleeping off the boredom less now that I had something to stay up for. I didn't need the rest, but unconsciousness beat counting tiles hands down. To stop me complaining about the mind-numbing dullness when he wasn't around, we tried an experiment where he taped the magazine pages to one of the walls so I could read them after he'd gone, but one of the cleaners took them down, muttering darkly about weirdo vandals and stake-outs. Not wanting to be arrested, Jeremy refused to do it again.

On his next visit, I couldn't help noticing he looked pretty pleased with himself.

'OK. Out with it,' I gave in finally. 'What's with the smugness?'

'I have news.'

'I know, I'm reading it. Turn the page, please.'

He leaned against the wall. 'I've made a friend.'

I clasped my hands together. 'Lucky you. How many does that make? Two?'

Ignoring my sarcasm, he went on. 'I got talking to her at the theatre. She's a researcher for some supernatural TV programme that wants to shoot there, but more importantly, she claims she's psychic.'

He had my attention. 'In what way? Is she properly psychic, or does she just think she is?'

Jeremy shrugged. 'I haven't a clue. Some of the stuff she came out with was a bit peculiar. It was only when she mentioned a spiritualist church they'd filmed at that I paid attention.'

I knew next to nothing about spiritualism, but anyone

who told someone they'd just met that they spoke to the dead was plain weird in my opinion.

'You didn't tell her about me, did you?'

'Of course. I came right out with it – "There's this girl I see who no one else does, and I turn the pages for her because she can't hold a newspaper".' He fixed me with a level stare. 'Believe it or not, I'm not totally comfortable with this myself yet.'

I bit back a smile. At least we agreed on one thing.

'What happens at these churches, then?'

'People go along to speak to their dead family and friends. Apparently, it's teeming with the souls of the departed all looking for ways to "pass across".' He did that rubbishy thing adults do with their fingers to indicate speech marks. 'I wondered if you wanted me to go along and see what I can find out.'

'You'd do that for me?' I was genuinely taken aback. There were people I'd known my whole life who wouldn't put themselves out as much. 'Why?'

Jeremy looked pointedly into cubicle one, where the friendly neighbourhood vandals had stuffed so much toilet roll into the bowl that it was overflowing. 'Since I seem to be the only one who can see you, I feel responsible for you, and much as I enjoy spending my evenings in a public toilet, I think it might be a good idea to find a way to get you out of here.'

He wouldn't get any complaints from me. Even so, it meant a lot that he'd go to such an effort when he could easily walk away and never see me again.

'Well, thanks.' In case he thought I was getting all mushy on him, I added, 'Don't go thinking that means we're proper mates or anything.'

Satisfied we understood each other, I turned my attention to the gossip columns. Surely that Hollywood couple weren't adopting another baby?

'Do you know why I really came back?' Jeremy's voice was soft.

Sensing he was about to reveal something, I glanced up. 'My charming personality?'

A brief smile flickered over his face. 'When you were watching me in the mirror, your expression reminded me of someone else. A few years ago, I was at Camden tube station one night when the woman next to me threw herself in front of the train. In the split second before she jumped her eyes met mine.' Swallowing hard, he shook his head. 'You looked like her, pleading for someone to understand how you felt. No one deserves to be so alone.'

Tears swam into my eyes. I blinked them away. 'It's all right once you get used to it. Sitting through double science was worse.'

The spell broke. 'I almost believe you. Why don't I fill you in on last night's *EastEnders*?'

Grateful for the change of subject, I listened and didn't correct him when he got the characters mixed up. He was an adult and deeply uncool, but somehow it didn't matter. He cared enough to keep coming back to me. Right at that moment, it was all I had.

Chapter 3

'They said what?'

I couldn't believe my ears. If this was Jeremy's idea of a joke, he was an even worse comedian than my dad.

One eyebrow raised, he spread the paper he'd brought across the sink. I approached without much enthusiasm. *The Times* wasn't on my list of acceptable reading matter.

'I'm only telling you what the woman at the Church of the Dearly Departed told me. Spirits can escape their earthly prison – that's here for you – as long as they have something from that place with them when they go. Anything will do.'

I glanced around. 'What did you have in mind? Reckon you could wrench a loo-roll holder off the wall for me to carry around?'

Jeremy frowned. 'Of course not. Something a bit more portable would be better. A toilet brush, maybe?' His gaze came to rest on the door of cubicle one. 'Didn't you say vandals had knocked the toilet seat off in there?'

They had, late one night as I'd been snoozing in my cupboard. The racket had scared the bejaysus out of me, but they'd been oblivious to my terrified scream and had only run off after the plumbing had started making ominous creaking noises. I eyed the door doubtfully. As much as I longed to get back out into the real world, was Jeremy seriously suggesting that I take a loo seat out with me?

'I don't care if no one else can see it. If you think for one minute I'm going out in public wearing that you've got another thing coming. I do have some pride.' Another thought occurred to me. 'Anyway, Brainiac, how am I supposed to hold on to it?'

To prove my point, I waved my arm through the wall.

He shrugged. 'I don't know. She was a bit hazy on the details.'

Probably because she was making them up as she went along. 'What else did she say?'

Jeremy unfolded the lightweight chair he'd brought with him and sat down.

'That ghosts are the souls of people with unfinished business on earth, seeking a way to get to the next plane of existence.'

I opened my mouth to make a smart remark about airports and closed it again. It was good of Jeremy to find this stuff out. If I ever wanted to see the shops again, I needed to keep him sweet.

'And did she give you any hints about how I'm supposed to do that?' I said.

He threw me an uneasy look. 'You resolve whatever is keeping you here. In your case, that means finding the person who killed you, I expect.'

My stomach tightened with sudden anxiety. That was Rule Number Two: Never Think About What Happened Last New Year's Eve. It was cowardly, but I preferred not to dwell on the manner of my death.

Seeing my reluctance, Jeremy changed tack. 'We could always try getting you exorcised.'

I rolled my eyes and hid behind sarcasm. 'Look at me, Jeremy. Weight gain is not currently an issue.'

He smirked. 'Not exercised. Exorcised. As in a priest comes and banishes you.'

I'd seen a horror movie once. GCSE Occultism it wasn't. How was I supposed to know all these bizarre terms? Whatever it was, it sounded charming. 'Why didn't you mention it earlier? Do I get a choice where I'm banished to, or is it generally to the pits of hell?'

Jeremy got to his feet. 'You're in a bad mood. Why don't we concentrate on finding you something to wear? It's about time you had a change of scene.'

I don't know if you've ever tried to accessorise with only the contents of a public lavatory to choose from, but let me tell you, it's not blimmin' easy. We are not talking Claire's

19

Accessories here. Call me picky, but I'm not convinced lavvy-chic is ever going to catch on.

'Are you sure about this?' I cast a dubious glance around the cleaner's cupboard. The gigantic spider in the corner fixed me with an evil stare from his industrial-strength lair. Sadly, death hadn't cured me of my knee-wobbling terror of the eight-legged monsters, and he kept me awake on numerous occasions by creeping around the shelves. I think he enjoyed it. Whoever said spiders were more scared of us than we were of them couldn't have met the Beast of the Bog.

'There must be something in there you can use. Isn't there an overall or something?'

I stuck my head out and adopted a petulant expression. 'It's no good. I haven't a thing to wear.'

Jeremy raised a disbelieving eyebrow. 'What, nothing at all?'

'*Nada.*' I studied the cupboard interior again. 'Except for the most tragic pair of lime-green jogging bottoms I've ever seen, and there's more chance of my mum's hairdresser declaring he's straight than there is of me being seen dead in those babies.'

He tapped on the door, making me jump. I hadn't heard him approach.

'No one can see you except me, and I promise not to laugh. Close your eyes and pretend they're Prada.'

I heaved an unhappy sigh and scowled down at the jogging bottoms. Someone, somewhere, was going to pay for this.

'All right, Mr Style Guru. How, exactly, do you suggest I get them on?'

Unfortunately for me, it was easier than I thought. My fingers floated through the material just as I'd expected, but when I pulled, the trousers came with them. I grimaced at them for a moment, unsure whether to be pleased or disgusted, before poking an experimental foot through one leg hole. The other followed. Disgust won. By some extraordinary design fault, the trousers were too tight around the knee and ballooned to mammoth proportions around the waist.

I had to hand it to Jeremy. Not a peep escaped him when I finally edged out of the cupboard. The horrified silence said it all.

'I'm stuck here for eternity.' I waved a miserable hand at my frog legs. 'I cannot go out in these. My bum looks the size of a small planet.'

'They're not that bad.' Jeremy sounded as convincing as a lap-dancer auditioning for the part of the Virgin Mary. 'And it's not as though anyone but me can see them.'

My nose wrinkled in disgust. 'They stink of bleach.'

Jeremy tilted his head sideways. 'Look on the bright side. They might just be your ticket out of here.' He extended an arm to me, like I was a Victorian lady. 'Shall we?'

I swallowed. Now that it came down to it, I was nervous. The toilets might not be the Ritz, but they were relatively quiet and hardly anyone walked through me. Forgetting for

21

a moment the fact that I resembled an upside-down pear, how was I going to cope with the crowds of gormless tourists who hung around Carnaby Street at all hours of the day and night?

'Come on, Kermit.' Jeremy jerked his head towards the stairs. 'How bad can it be?'

Think of the worst, most unpleasant cross-country run you've ever done. Your lungs are burning, you're certain you're going to throw up and there's no end in sight. Imagine you're doing this in a gale force wind and your ears are about to pop horribly. Hold on to that thought and you might have some idea of how it feels when someone walks through you. Multiply it by around ten and you'll know how I felt on my way through Leicester Square.

'I hate you.' I backed away from the kerb and shot Jeremy a weakly venomous glare. 'I'm going to follow you home and haunt you.'

Not wanting to come across as a raving lunatic by apparently talking to himself in front of several hundred people, Jeremy responded with a pointed glance at my hated leg-wear.

'You don't think I can be scary dressed like this? How about if I sang to you? Twenty-four seven.' I pitched my voice as high as it would go. '*Oooohhhh baaaby, you're the bessst . . .*'

Jeremy's eyes took on a pinched look and he hastily interrupted my tuneless wailing. 'I think that's enough exercise for one evening.'

The red-faced man on his left turned mournfully towards him. 'Speak for yourself, mate. The doctor says I need to shift another ten pounds.'

'Ten?' I scoffed as we dodged down the less crowded side streets back to Carnaby Street. 'Twenty, more like it.'

Jeremy didn't speak again until we reached the entrance to my toilet.

'Are you really going to torture me with non-stop boy band lyrics?'

I shuffled my feet. The journey back hadn't been so bad, once I'd worked out a shuffle-hop system to dodge people. Maybe I was getting used to being invisible.

'It depends on whether you keep on with the muppet jokes.'

'If I could find out more about the Church of the Dearly Departed, would you like to go along one evening? I could organise a night off work.'

My eyes narrowed in thought. If tonight was anything to go by, getting around would become easier with time, and I had to admit I was curious. What did spiritualists get up to, anyway? A year ago, I'd have laughed at the idea of people talking to ghosts. I wasn't laughing at all now.

'Yeah, all right. I'm up for it if you are.'

He nodded, looking pleased. 'Well done tonight. I know it wasn't easy.'

I stood at the top of the stairs after he'd gone, watching the living go about the business of enjoying themselves in the cool night air. Six months ago I was one of them, laughing and joking with my mates, unaware that I'd soon be nothing more than a spectator. Part of me wanted to try and warn them to seize the moment, tell their friends and family they loved them before it was too late. Instead, I swallowed my sudden wave of misery and trudged down the stairs to my cupboard. It wasn't much consolation, but at least I could part company with the puke-coloured pants.

Chapter 4

The Church of the Dearly Departed was in Kensal Green, which meant a trip on the dreaded Underground. Although the prospect made me feel sick, the reality wasn't so bad. I even got a seat, which had almost never happened when I was alive, and no one sat on me. Thanks to Jeremy's brainwave of threading my neck chain through an old rubber plug from a stock I found in the cupboard, at least I no longer looked like a bag lady's less fashionable sister. I'd considered hiding it in my pocket but the nasty bulge it made in my super skinny jeans cured me of that idea. Besides, it felt more secure around my neck and became part of me, like a sort of cheapo necklace. It made going out in public a lot more bearable, for me at any rate. Jeremy, on the other hand, had to put up with my stream of comments about our fellow passengers, none of which he was able to answer in the busy carriage. He seemed to be bearing up well.

'I mean, seriously, no one wears Converse with shorts. They make your feet look massive and those black socks are a definite fashion no-no —'

'For the love of God, will you shut up!' Reaching the end of his patience, Jeremy bellowed at me across the carriage. Meekly, I did as I was told and watched as, red-faced and fuming, he subsided into his seat. A lot of passengers changed carriage at the next station.

'What time does it start?' I asked, once we were free of the crowds and making our way along the street.

'Sen-hurty.' Ever conscious of drawing attention to himself, Jeremy hissed the words from the corner of his mouth. I totally understood his concern. It wasn't the kind of neighbourhood you wanted to get noticed in.

'Are we nearly there yet? I'm not used to all this walking.'

His response was a single grunt.

'Do you think we should have got a taxi or something? I'm really not up for – whoa!'

Rounding the corner, we came to an abrupt halt. Directly across the road stood a modern red-brick building, with an enormous sign reading *Church of the Dearly Departed*. Queuing patiently outside was the biggest congregation I'd ever seen.

'It must be some service,' I breathed. 'Last time I saw a crowd like this the Ra Ra Ras were rocking Islington Academy.'

I caught Jeremy giving me a strange sideways glance, but I was already moving forward, intrigued about the big attraction. 'Come on, let's join the line.'

'Or we could go straight in?'

I tutted. 'How rude would that be? Didn't your mum teach you any manners?'

Frowning, Jeremy said, 'Rude to who? We'll miss the start if we don't get in there now.'

My gaze strayed to the mass of people in front of me. 'They won't start with half their congregation on the pavement.'

'What are you talking about?' he shook his head, puzzled. 'Everyone's gone in apart from us.'

I looked hard at him. 'Jeremy, how many people can you see?'

He stared back. 'Is this a trick question?'

'Tell me you can see the girl in the blue dress over there, and the old man with the walking stick?'

Confused, he shook his head. 'There's only you and me.'

I'd heard enough. 'Excuse me.' I stepped forward and spoke to a slender, ebony-skinned girl of around my age. 'Are you here for the spiritualist service?'

She looked up from her phone and rolled her eyes. 'Duh. Why else would I be here? No one else is going to pay me any attention.'

You didn't have to be Einstein to work out that something odd was going on. If I looked hard enough, I could make out the faintest blue tinge around some of the people.

I'd been dead a few months but, as far as I remembered, the living didn't glow. The penny dropped.

I turned to Jeremy excitedly. 'There are other ghosts here. I guess you can only see me.'

His eyes darted sideways. 'Why can't I see them?'

'Maybe you're not psychic enough?'

He shifted uneasily. 'And they're here, right now?'

Nodding, I took a good look around for myself. Now that I knew what was going on, some of the things which had been jumping up and down begging to be noticed fell into place. For a start, the mix of people was too weird for words. There were young, old, and everything in between, including – hurrah – teens. From what I could tell, a range of nationalities seemed to be represented, too. One man was carrying a kettle, another had a pair of garden shears. My gaze rested on a grown man dressed up as a baby. I didn't want to know what that was about.

'I think I'd better go in first. We don't want you standing on anyone's toes.'

Still glancing from side to side, Jeremy agreed and followed my lead as I joined the throng. I had no idea what was going to happen in there, but whatever it was, it certainly pulled in the punters.

Inside, an expectant hush descended over the waiting mixture of the living and the dead. We squeezed in at the back, where it was standing room only with more people still to come in. I savoured the new sensation of brushing up against the other ghosts, and smiled apologetically as I accidentally nudged the chubby, heavily made-up Emo girl beside me. She didn't smile back. Instead, she blew an enormous bubble. It popped loudly.

'Dearly beloved.' A strong voice echoed through the buzzing air as a white-robed minister climbed into the pulpit and spread his arms. 'Dearly departed. Welcome, one and all!'

The answering calls were deafening. For some of my fellow ghosts, it was clear that the relief of being heard was too much to bear. A woman in front of me broke down in tears.

'Can you hear them?' I whispered to Jeremy.

He shrugged. 'A few voices. Any chance of a seat? There are loads of empty pews.'

Scanning the packed benches, I replied with a sharp shake of my head. 'You can't plonk yourself on the lap of someone you've never met. Honestly, I worry about you sometimes.'

'Would it hurt?'

'Not you, unless I find a way to smack you around the ear, but it wouldn't be a picnic for the ghost.'

The minister went on. 'Do we have any amongst us who seeks answer this evening?'

Once again, the roar of voices swelled as hundreds clamoured to be noticed. I craned my neck to see what was going on at the front.

'What's happening?' I hissed.

Emo girl threw me a shark-eyed look through her

straggly, jet-black fringe. 'Are you going to talk all the way through? It's no skin off my nose, but there are other people trying to listen.'

Feeling the burn of embarrassment rising up my cheeks, I waved my hands in apology. 'Sorry. It's my first time here. I haven't really got the hang of it yet.'

Seemingly satisfied, she jerked her head towards Jeremy. 'Dunno why you'd bother. It looks like you've got your own psychic anyway.'

'Haven't you?' It crossed my mind that I might be very lucky to have someone who could see me.

'Shhh!' An elderly woman dressed in a hideous floral tent glared at us ferociously.

Emo girl considered me for a moment, then pointed outside. I leaned across to Jeremy. 'I'm going to find out what's going on. Stay here and do not sit on anyone.'

We threaded our way through the congregation and outside into the falling dusk. I was amazed to see more ghosts had arrived.

'It's popular here.'

The girl shrugged. 'Not everyone's as lucky as you. Word about the Dearly D gets around. This is the only way some of us can get a message through to the living.'

She sounded as though she spoke from bitter experience.

'Is that why you're here? My name's Lucy, by the way.'

'I'm Hep. And no, I haven't got anything earth-shattering to say to the world. I'm just here for the vibe.'

I nodded, wondering what to say next. I was torn

between curiosity about the church and wanting to know about my new friend. She was the first ghost I'd really talked to. Were there rules to be observed? Maybe it was rude to ask her how she'd died.

'So. How did you go?' she said.

Oh. Obviously not. I took a deep breath and tried to sound casual. 'Murdered. You?'

Her eyes glittered with interest. She pulled a thick coil of rope from under the neck of her jumper and waved it at me. 'Suicide.'

Once again, I didn't know what to say. The Emos I'd known at school were notoriously unstable, but no one I knew had tried to kill themselves. I wondered whether she'd actually meant to die or intended it to be a cry for attention. Did I dare ask?

In the end, I bottled it and changed the subject. 'What gives with the live ones? Do they come here to find out stuff from their dead loved ones?'

Hep snapped her bubble gum, looking bored. 'Yeah. The mediums here are really good. Dead people come from miles around but hardly any of them get a word in. The psychics get tired out really fast when everyone shouts at once.'

Her relentless chewing fascinated me. 'Did you have that gum when you died?'

She blew another bubble, nodding. 'Cola-flavoured Hubba Bubba. Not that it's got much flavour left after a year.' Her eyes narrowed. 'Where did you find Droopy? He looks like he doesn't get out much.'

Something about the way she said it made me think she wasn't as dismissive as she was trying to make out. 'Jeremy? He's all right, for an old bloke. He's the reason I'm here.'

She kicked at a stone with a heavy Doc Marten boot. It bounced away into the road. 'Can he see anyone else?'

'Not so far. He thinks the church is half empty.' I watched as she took aim at a discarded Coke can. Realisation dawned. 'You just kicked that stone!'

Hep scowled. 'Yeah? There's no law against it.'

Excitement fizzed inside me. 'You can touch things. How do you do that?'

'Blimey, you really are a newbie, aren't you?' A grin split her pale face. She was much less scary when she smiled. 'It's easy. Pull up a chair and I'll show you how it's done.'

Chapter 5

If you've ever watched a supposed ghost documentary, you'll know there's more than one flavour of ghost. Some are the standard *Scooby Doo* spooks, who wave their arms around and moan all the time. Then there are those who choose to spend eternity nicking anything that isn't nailed down and hiding it so they can watch the living tear their hair out looking for their stuff. I once blamed my missing RE homework on ghostly goings-on. It earned me a detention and an appointment with the Deputy Head.

Hep wasn't either of those. She was a poltergeist, the kind who loved to throw things. I suppose as an Emo she must have been pretty close to the emotional edge when she was alive, so it made perfect sense that her feelings still ran high after death. Whatever the reason, Hep was one angry spectre, and she'd learned how to channel that fury to move things around, often violently.

'The secret is to focus completely on what you want to move,' she advised as I prodded without success at a fast food carton on the ground. 'If you really want it, you can make bits of yourself solid long enough to manipulate things. It's easier if you draw on a strong emotion.'

I imagined a disembodied finger floating in front of me. 'Doesn't that freak out the living?'

She threw me a level look. 'Obviously we can't be seen or the entire world would believe in ghosts. Now, imagine your finger is a flick-knife and the stone is your worst enemy.'

'Are you always this bloodthirsty?' Lying flat out on the pavement with my tongue sticking out with concentration, I could just imagine what my old school bully would say if she could see me now. Something devastatingly witty, no doubt.

A sneering giggle floated through the air. 'Down in the gutter with the other crap, Hep? Or should I call you Rosemary?'

I frowned and pushed myself up. Who the flip was Rosemary?

'My name is Hepzibah,' Hep spat, her tone reaching new depths of surliness. 'Anyway, I'm surprised you can see who you're talking to with your head stuck so far up your arse.'

I turned round. In front of me was the most gorgeous pair of turquoise sandals. My gaze travelled upwards to a sickeningly pretty blonde straight out of an American teen comedy. She was flanked on either side by a wannabe. I'd met her type before and shook my head incredulously. It seemed even the afterlife had a queen bee.

Deciding to give her a chance to prove me wrong, I smiled. 'Hi. I'm Lucy.'

The girl gazed down at me, her perfect rosebud lips twisting in disdain. 'And what have we here? Don't tell me the freak's got herself a girlfriend.'

Steeling myself, I got to my feet and prepared to bite back.

'Why didn't anyone tell me Barbie had died?' I shook my head sorrowfully. 'Poor Ken. How will he cope?'

OK, it was hardly comedy genius, but at least I'd stood my ground.

Looking my black skinny jeans and grey denim waistcoat up and down, it was a moment before the girl spoke. 'If you're smart, you'll learn that anyone who hangs around with losers like Ginger here is the lowest of the low.' She tossed her hair and turned to her attendants. 'Come on, let's see if Ryan's around.'

Scornfully, I watched them leave. 'Nice shoes, shame about the wearer.'

Hep's forehead creased into a murderous glower. 'Kimberly Jones. She likes to think she's special, but she's stuck here the same as the rest of us.'

'I've seen her type before. Don't let her get you down.' I waved a dismissive hand. 'She didn't even make sense. You're not ginger.'

Scowl deepening further, Hep said, 'I was before I dyed

my hair. Pity I didn't think about touching up my roots before I killed myself. See?' Her head dipped to display her parting. Above the black there were two centimetres of unmistakeable ginger. 'How was I supposed to know I'd be stuck with them forever?'

It was a fair question. I'd been on my way home from a party when I'd died and looked pretty damn hot, if I said so myself. Sadly, the dice hadn't rolled so generously for Hep. I decided to change the subject. 'Who's Ryan?'

Her face softened. 'Ryan's all right. He's about our age, died in a car crash, but you'd never know it to look at him.' She grimaced. 'Kimberly would love to call herself his girl-friend, but she's not his type.'

The words made me think. I hadn't considered that as a ghost I still had a chance at a love life. Now that I knew ghosts could touch each other, questions were queuing up for answers. Was it easy to hold their hand? Come to think of it, did it feel the same when you snogged them? It was becoming apparent there was a lot I didn't know.

'Right,' I said, nodding. 'Who's Rosemary?'

She was silent for so long I thought she wasn't going to reply at all. When she finally did speak, it was through gritted teeth. 'My stupid parents thought I looked like my great aunt and named me after her.' She shook her head in fury. 'And people wonder why I committed suicide. At least now I can be called whatever I want.'

It didn't seem to me that being called Rosemary was reason enough to take your own life, but who was I to argue? I'd always liked my name. Even so, I imagined there was a lot more to it than Hep was letting on, but it wasn't the kind of conversation you have with someone you've only just met. Once again, I took the easy escape. 'Tell me again how to move this carton?'

After twenty minutes of sweat-breaking concentration, I still couldn't shift it and my frustration was starting to show.

'It takes time,' Hep commented as I collapsed into a groaning heap. 'Nobody gets it on their first try.'

I heaved a melodramatic sigh. 'But I've got my heart set on a job at the celestial drive-thru.'

She smiled. 'I didn't realise you were the ambitious type. Give it a rest now and try again tomorrow. You'll get there in the end.'

Knowing she was right didn't make me feel any better. If I had one fault, it was not knowing when to give up. Like when I'd demanded ballet lessons at the age of four and persevered until the age of seven, even after it became painfully clear I had three left feet. My mother, bless her, had never once suggested I give up. She'd been great like that. I missed her.

Reluctantly, I climbed to my feet. Seconds later I wished I hadn't as Hep and the church swam before my eyes. I swayed, blinking furiously until my vision cleared.

Hep reached out to steady me. Her hands settled on my arms. 'Are you OK?'

I didn't know. For a moment, I'd thought I was going to faint, the way I had last year when I'd tried to survive on a diet of sunflower seeds and grapefruit. That had come to an abrupt end after I collapsed in assembly. I couldn't blame my diet this time, though. Ghosts don't eat. 'I think so. Everything went a bit weird then.'

Hep let go and moved her pallid face closer to mine. 'How long have you been away from home?'

Who'd have thought I'd ever consider a public toilet home? 'Dunno. A few hours, I suppose?'

She pulled out her mobile and checked the time. 'You'd better head home, unless you want your return trip to be a whole lot less pleasant than the one here.'

Puzzled, I frowned at her. 'Why?'

'God save me from newbs.' Her eyes shot skywards. 'You're tied to the place where you died. Taking something from that place will allow you to leave for a while, but since you're new to the experience, it won't be very long before you need to recharge. If you don't, eventually you'll be dragged back, and believe me, you don't want to go through that.'

Judging from the way she shuddered, she'd been there, and I was more than happy to accept her word that it was no picnic. 'I'd better find Jeremy.'

'Yeah, you do that.' Hep tapped her phone thoughtfully. 'Even if he's only a little bit psychic, he might turn out to be useful. You should give me your mobile number so we can hook up here next week.'

* * *

I wondered what she meant the entire journey home. Not about the phone number: once I'd left the toilet I noticed I got a signal and Hep explained about the weird ghostly network the dead used. Obviously we couldn't contact the living, else people wouldn't be able to move for messages from the dead, but inter-spirit texting and calls were apparently OK. Once I'd got over my surprise that there was a Network Spooky, I liked what I heard. Unlimited talk-time and all the texts you could send? If I ever made any more ghostly mates, we could have a text-fest.

What I didn't get was her comment about Jeremy. He wasn't bad company, and he was very handy in the magazine department, but he couldn't see Hep, or any other ghosts for that matter. She didn't strike me as the needy type. How she expected him to be of any practical use was anyone's guess.

Chapter 6

'Fancy a tour of the theatre?' Jeremy asked casually a few days after our trip to the church. 'I've got to check all the lighting rigs before the show starts so I'm going in early. You can come along if you like.'

I didn't have a better offer. Thanks to Jeremy's half-brained insistence that I go out regularly 'for a breath of fresh air', I was now an old hand at avoiding gormless tourists and could stay away from home for at least four hours at a stretch without feeling faint. Hep boasted she managed six times as long. Since our trip to the Dearly D, a whole new world had opened up to me, and Hep was the best part of it. I'd met other teen ghosts, but Hep and I had clicked, in spite of our radical differences. She was proving surprisingly patient at answering my gazillion questions about being dead. On the whole, things were looking up. I even ventured out without Jeremy from time to time. I didn't tell him about that. He liked to feel needed.

The theatre was one of those fantastic old buildings that you somehow become blind to when you live in London. The reddish-brown sandstone was dirty from the daily pollution but I thought it just added to the air of faded glory. Inside, it was all deep red carpets and gilt mirrors. The current production was an Abba tribute show.

'Is it any good?'

Jeremy pulled a face. 'It was OK the first few times. I've seen about seven hundred performances now so it's not exactly fresh. I could sing it in my sleep.'

The image of Jeremy flat on his back crooning *Gimme, Gimme, Gimme* made me smile. 'Bet that makes you an exciting bed-mate, then.'

He shook his head firmly. 'That's not a conversation I'm having with you.'

I thought about that as we dodged along the packed streets. 'I can't believe I haven't asked you about your love life. I just imagined you were single. Maybe it's your dress sense.'

Lips quirking into a wry smile, he didn't answer.

Something else occurred to me. 'Do you still live with your parents? Not that there's anything wrong with it if you do.'

This earned me a level stare and I decided to shut up.

Once we were safely tucked away in the lighting box, Jeremy wasted no time setting me straight. 'No, I don't live with my parents. They live in Norwich. And I am single, which is lucky for you because she'd have to be a very understanding woman to accept that I spend most of my spare time hanging around the toilets in Carnaby Street.'

Urgh. I hadn't given much thought to how that sounded. He was lucky he hadn't been arrested. 'OK, sorry I asked.'

'So you should be. Come on. If you're really lucky you'll meet the psychotic theatre cat.'

I half expected the theatre to be already haunted, but if it was, the resident ghost kept well out of my way as Jeremy scaled a towering portable ladder to check the conditions of the lights above the auditorium and stage. By the time he'd finished, other employees were starting to arrive, forcing us back to the lighting box where at least Jeremy could answer my questions.

I was thrilled when he agreed that I could stay for the show.

'Thanks! I promise I'll be quiet.'

His expression suggested he found that hard to believe. I was on my best behaviour, though, and only distracted him once in the show. He made a big deal out of it. Personally, I don't think anyone in the audience would have noticed the late spotlight during the leading lady's solo. It dawned on me, as he flipped levers and pushed buttons on the complicated lighting desk, that he was quite good at his job. By the end of the show, I was almost eyeing him with respect. I didn't mention it, naturally. He might start thinking I liked him or something.

'If you give me a minute to finish up, I'll walk you home.'

I rolled my eyes. 'Right, cos something bad might happen to me otherwise.'

Jeremy's gaze was steady. 'All the same, I'd be happier seeing you safely back to your cupboard.'

I was trying to come up with a smart comment when a tap at the door interrupted my thoughts. Jeremy threw me a warning glance.

'Come in.'

A woman with a long thin nose and vibrant purple hair poked her head round the door. 'Hi, Jeremy. Tonight's the night we start filming. We're setting up infra-red cameras in the auditorium to catch any supernatural activity. Any chance you could help?' She paused, nose ring twitching suspiciously as she peered around the tiny room. 'I could have sworn I heard you talking to someone.'

'Myself. I often do.' He threw her an uneasy grimace. 'It's the only way I get the answer I want. Do you need me right now?'

The woman's eyes slid sideways, as though she didn't believe him. 'Yes please. By the way, the big cheese was looking for you.'

'The director? Did he say why?'

She raised a pierced eyebrow and smiled thinly. 'No, but

I expect it's got something to do with Serena singing half her big solo in the dark.'

Jeremy climbed gloomily to his feet. 'I'd better not keep him waiting then, or there'll be one more ghost for you to catch on camera. Thanks for the heads up, Elvira.'

I snorted with laughter. Elvira? Talk about a lame attempt at sounding cool. She was at least forty years old. Minus the purple hair and multiple piercings, she'd look more like an Eileen. I stuck my head out of the door and watched them make their way along the corridor.

'Don't be long,' I called at Jeremy's retreating back. 'And watch out for the human pincushion. She looks prickly.'

Elvira stiffened and turned her head slightly, as though she'd heard something. Too late, I remembered Jeremy had mentioned there was a psychic on the TV production team. I wouldn't mind betting he'd been talking about Elvira. Thoughtfully, I pulled my head back into the lighting box. She couldn't see me, but it was possible she could hear me, and I had an uneasy feeling about her. The last thing I wanted was to be the star of her cheesy TV show. I'd have to remember to keep it zipped if I ever bumped into her again.

That turned out to be sooner than I expected. I'd sat in Jeremy's seat and was concentrating on moving one of the sliders when the door swung open and Elvira came in. In her arms was a sleek, black cat.

Now don't get me wrong, I have nothing against cats. My nan had one and I got along with it just fine. The one Elvira was carrying wasn't anything like Mr Cuddles, though, and judging from the way it was hissing at me, with its ears flat against its head, I had a sneaking suspicion it could see me. That wasn't a problem in itself – unless Elvira was an extremely unlikely-looking Dr Dolittle, the cat wasn't going to be talking – but I couldn't shake the feeling she'd expected this reaction. That could only mean she suspected I was there.

'What is it, Lucy?' she crooned, lips resting against the cat's furry ears.

I froze. Now that was seriously spooky. How in hell's teeth did she know my name?

'Is there a disgusting ghost in here?' She shuddered, a look of revulsion on her face. 'We hate ghosts, don't we, Lucifer?'

The breath whooshed out of me. Who in their right mind names their cat after the devil *and brings it to work*? Wait . . . hadn't Jeremy said something about a theatre cat? I relaxed slightly. OK, so she wasn't some all-knowing witch after all, but she was still freaking me out. I had to get rid of her. Desperately, I thought back to those long Sunday afternoons at Nan's. My cousins took great delight in jumping out at Mr Cuddles when he least expected it, causing the cat to leap upwards and claw at anything within reach. I narrowed my eyes in thought. Perched in Elvira's arms, Lucifer did not look like a happy feline. His barely contained temper gave me an idea.

I levelled my most intimidating stare deep into the cat's amber eyes. 'Boo!'

The air was filled with a furious yowling as Lucifer morphed into a spitting, scratching furball. Elvira screamed, a shrill screech of agony, and dropped him. He wasted no time legging it and shot from the room. Whimpering, and nursing some vicious-looking scratches to her neck and face, Elvira threw an evil glare around the room.

'I can sense you're here,' she hissed. 'It's only a matter of time until we catch you, one way or another.'

With one final scowl she was gone, leaving me shaking like I'd just had a run-in with the biggest bully in the playground. What exactly did she mean – catch me? On film, or did she mean something else? My mind flicked back to an old re-run of *Ghostbusters* I'd seen where the ghosts had been snared with lasers or something – I definitely didn't fancy being trapped for eternity or whatever else Cruella de Vil had in mind. I shivered and wrapped my arms around myself. The whole experience had been too close for comfort. The moment Jeremy came back, I was so out of there.

Chapter 7

The next time I dragged Jeremy to the Dearly D, three days later, Hep tried not to be impressed when I sent two empty fries packets and a Coke can sailing into the bin. 'It took me ages to move even a crisp packet and I had a head-start in the anger stakes. How did you learn so quickly?'

I didn't tell her I'd spent a whole morning stabbing at a dubious ball of tissue I'd discovered on the floor in one of the cubicles. There were some things no one needed to know, and I didn't want to come across as Little Miss Competitive. 'Practice, I suppose. My social life isn't exactly blistering, y'know.'

It was true. Since my encounter with Elvira and the satanic moggy, both Jeremy and I thought it was too dangerous for me to spend any more time at the theatre.

Whatever her plans were, I couldn't risk running into her again. Bang went my idea of becoming some kind of angelic lighting technician. It wasn't as though I had a bulging contact list to ring round when I got bored.

Hep made a passable stab at a smile. 'Well, this should cheer you up. Ryan is throwing a party this weekend, and you're invited.'

She was right. My mood instantly lifted. 'How does he know who I am? Did Kimberly tell him?'

Hep shook her head. 'I think it's safe to say that Kimberly hasn't described you in flattering terms. You have me to thank for your invitation. I asked Ryan whether it was OK if you tagged along. He said yes.'

I was genuinely touched. 'Thanks, Hep. I'd love to go with you.'

'Hadn't you better ask your dad?' She jerked her head towards the church, where Jeremy was enduring another service on my behalf. He found the people there interesting, he said, although often sad. Personally, I couldn't bear the desperation in the air.

'Nah. He'll be cool with it. You'll see.'

'I'm sorry, Lucy, I don't think it's a good idea.'

I couldn't believe this was happening. I'd mentioned the party once we were safely back home, expecting him to nod approvingly. Instead, Jeremy had gone off the deep end. Do not pass go, do not collect two hundred pounds, go directly to ridiculously over-protective mode. There weren't many

48

upsides to being dead, but surely being free from stupid adult rules had to be one of them. So why was I being told what to do by someone I'd known less than two months? It didn't seem fair.

'I've been invited to a party and I want to go. Why is that so difficult to understand?'

Jeremy shrugged. 'It's not. But you don't know these people very well. What if something goes wrong?'

I stared, exasperated. 'What could possibly happen?'

'There are more ways to hurt someone than just physically.' He shook his head doubtfully. 'I think I should come too.'

I groaned. Things were getting worse. 'You *cannot* do this to me. Even my own parents were never this cruel.'

'We know there are other people who can sense your presence, Lucy.' He threw me a pleading look. 'I'm only looking out for you.'

He meant well, but it didn't make me feel any better. My first party in the afterlife, and I was being babysat by a twenty-seven-year-old who dressed like someone twice his age. Did he have any idea how galactically uncool he was going to make me look?

It took five minutes of intense, moody silence to make him crack. 'If it helps, I won't come to the actual party. I'll find a pub nearby and you can come and find me when you're ready to go home.'

Remembering how much he'd done for me, I decided to call a truce. 'Fine. Don't think I'll give in and invite you to the party. It wouldn't be much fun for you anyway – I'd be the only one you could see.'

He grinned, evidently pleased that he'd got his way. 'Don't worry. I won't cramp your style.'

I raised a stern eyebrow. Or at least I tried to. It wasn't a skill I'd managed to master while alive, and my lack of physical form wasn't making it any easier. 'You'd better not, or it'll be non-stop pop for you. Choose wisely.'

By the time Saturday night came round, I was in a state of extreme anticipation. Seriously, I hadn't been that excited since I'd spotted a member of a chart-topping boy band in our local Sainsbury's when I was eleven, and if that doesn't paint you a picture of my state of mind, nothing will. When I get like that, my mouth tends to go into overdrive, and this was no exception. Jeremy put up with my motor-mouth tendencies with a wry smile. It had become a little strained by the time the bus deposited us at the side of the North Circular Road in Edmonton.

'OK, you can go now.' I turned expectantly to Jeremy and wiggled my fingers in a cute little wave. 'Have fun.'

He didn't move. 'You haven't given me the address yet. How can I pick you up if I don't know where you are?'

I was beginning to wonder if there was some kind of joke going on. Jeremy could not possibly be expecting to pick me up. Any moment, a ghostly TV presenter with an inane grin was going to step through a wall and tell me I'd been set up.

'That is a very good question.' I folded my arms and adopted my most sincere expression. 'And the answer is that you're not. Tell me where you're going and I'll come and find you when I'm ready to head home.'

'All right.'

It was too easy. I blinked suspiciously. 'You're OK with that?'

He smiled. 'Of course. I'll just follow you to make sure you get there safely.'

I sighed, seeing where he was going. There was no way I wanted him trailing along behind me. 'The party is in a deserted factory behind that industrial estate over there.' I waved an arm towards the dark buildings silhouetted in the fading light. 'Hep says there's a pub beside those houses on the other side of the dual carriageway.'

'The last bus is just before midnight.' He glanced at his watch. 'Why don't we meet here at quarter to twelve?'

Nodding, I turned to go.

'Lucy?'

For the love of Marmite, what else did he have to say? Arranging my face into a patient expression, I turned around enquiringly.

'Stay off the spirits.' Chuckling at his own wit, he walked towards the passageway under the road.

'And you wonder why I don't want you to come with me.' Shaking my head in pity, I set off in the opposite direction.

Hep met me by the overgrown trail leading to the factory.

'You ditched your minder all right, then?'

'Yeah, wasn't sure I'd find this place though. What made Ryan have the party here?' I asked, picking my way through a sea of discarded beer cans, crisp packets and other rubbish. It was a long way from classy, but I don't suppose there are many places where the dead can let their hair down undisturbed.

Shrugging, Hep said, 'I think it's because he died near here. Did you see all the flowers by the roadside back there?'

I nodded. There had been a lot, and they'd looked fresh. I'd never paid much attention to things like that when I was alive. Now they told me that there was probably another member of my peculiar world nearby.

'His mum brings them every week,' she went on. 'It must have been really hard, losing her son and her husband at the same time.'

Death wasn't easy for anyone, I thought, but at least my parents had had each other, and my brother and sister. My mum had spent the weeks after my murder in my toilet, daring anyone to deny her access to fuss over flowers and talk to the empty air for hours. I swung from screaming anger to helpless sorrow as I struggled with the agony of not being able to reach her. More than anything, I battled for a way to tell her I was still there, listening to her broken-toned stories about the memorial assembly at school and the picture my bewildered little sister had drawn of me in heaven with the angels. The frustration was almost too much. Gradually, her visits lessened and in a way that helped me. It hurt too, until the last time she came with my dad and told me through streaming tears that they couldn't bear to use the streets where I had walked, or avoid my bedroom door any longer. The house where I'd once used my red felt tips to draw a giant dragon on the new wallpaper was sold. Gathering what was left of our tattered family close, they were moving away. I let them go, hollow with misery, knowing they were doing the right thing but unwilling to let go of the last shred of my life. Those weeks were the darkest I'd ever known.

'Hey, are you all right?' Hep's black-ringed eyes were concerned.

Never one to wallow in self-pity, I forced my memories to one side. 'Yeah, I'm fine.' Looking up at the broken windows of the factory, I put on my most sociable face. 'In the words of the song, let's get this party started.'

Chapter 8

Walking into that building was one of the hardest things I've ever done. Don't get me wrong, I'd been to plenty of parties in my fifteen years, but never without the comfort of knowing my mates had my back. Hep seemed OK, for an Emo. I had no idea if I could depend on her in a cuss fight.

I needn't have worried. She stuck to me like glue, pointing out the ghosts she knew and making me laugh with her sly comments about the ones she didn't especially like. Given her emotional state, that meant most of the party-goers.

The party itself looked amazing. Lanterns hung from hooks in the walls and tea lights were dotted on every available surface. Although it had been abandoned a long time ago, the fabric of the factory was still sound and most of the roof was intact. Here and there, a patch of orangey-blue city sky shone through, adding to the magical atmosphere. Fleetingly, I wondered how the candles had got there, but there were plenty of other things demanding my attention, not least of which was the music.

I flicked a head towards the centre of the room, where a band was thumping out crowd-pleasing tunes ranging from The Beatles to the latest floor-fillers. 'They're good. How come they've got their guitars?'

'Helicopter crash on their way back from Glastonbury a few years ago. We're lucky they weren't double-booked tonight.'

It hadn't crossed my mind that musicians would be in hot demand in the afterlife. 'Does Ryan know them?'

She nodded. 'He knows everyone.'

I was beginning to feel mighty curious about the wonderful Ryan. Reading my mind, Hep flashed me a faint smile. 'Come on, I'll introduce you to him.'

As I followed her through the crowd, I began to feel a worm of uneasiness creeping through me. He had a lot to live up to, this Ryan. What if he wasn't like I pictured him? What if he picked his nose or secretly liked *Star Trek* or talked like an utter chav? I bit my lip anxiously. What if he was the jock to Kimberly's cheerleader?

All of these worries melted away the moment I saw him. In the movie of my existence (which I'm imaginatively calling *The Life and Death of Lucy Shaw*), the crowds will part as I approach and he'll turn and be mesmerised by my total gorgeousness. Everyone will recognise that something wonderful has happened and will go and find something else to do, leaving us alone. He'll drop to one knee, gazing up at me in adoration. I'll say something sparkling, managing to be a cross between a glamorous Oscar-winning actress and a seeringly witty comedienne at the same time. Just so we're clear, it'll be the actress's looks and the comedienne's brains. Funny girls are all very well, but we all know who gets the A-list husbands.

Anyway, the reality didn't go quite so smoothly. For a start, Queen Kimberly was holding court around him, making it almost impossible to get close. Luckily, I had Hep with me, who simply elbowed her way in. I suppose you could say the crowd parted, in a shuffling kind of way. It would have been better if it hadn't closed immediately after her, leaving me stranded amongst hostiles.

'Excuse me,' I mumbled, trying the polite approach.

No one moved.

I tried again. 'Could I just squeeze through?'

Again, nothing. Maybe they couldn't hear me over the music. I was gathering in my breath, ready to let rip with a shout, when Hep's hand closed on my wrist and yanked me forwards through the bodies. I found myself face to face with The Perfect Boy.

'This is Lucy. She's new,' Hep said.

Ryan smiled, rows of white teeth sparkling against his tanned face. 'Hi.'

It's safe to say that in the Hollywood version of events, Ryan would be played by himself. Obviously this would depend on him not being dead, but you get the idea; he was film-star good-looking. His oh-so-casual sandy hair and deep blue eyes would have the entire female population of the planet staring up devotedly at pictures of him.

'Hng,' I said, in an effort to knock him sideways with my devastating charm. Unfortunately, my tongue seemed to be glued to the roof of my mouth. I peeled it away and tried again. 'Hi. Great party.'

He opened his mouth to reply, but Kimberly had spotted us. In an instant, she'd abandoned whoever she'd been talking to.

'Look, it's Rosie and her new playmate.' Her eyes glittered as she studied us. 'And they're holding hands. How sweet.'

Too late, I realised Hep was still holding on to my wrist. Lightning quick, she let go.

'So how long have you been here?' Ryan seemed not to have noticed Kimberly's comment.

Somehow, I knew he wasn't talking about the party. 'About eight months. You?'

'A year and a half.' Ruefully, he shrugged. 'I still don't know what I'm doing here.'

'You're here to make my afterlife bearable,' Kimberly said, her eyelashes fluttering up and down at speed.

I stared incredulously at her. 'Wow. I've read about that, but I've never seen anyone actually do it.'

She turned, smiling without a trace of humour. 'Do what?'

'Bat their eyelashes. You could probably get a job at a wind farm.'

'Ha ha.' Kimberly shot me a venomous look and turned her attention to Ryan. 'Come and dance with me.'

Easily, he shook his head. 'I'm talking to Lucy and Hep. Maybe later?'

It was one of those moments you store away to enjoy over and over when you're on your own with nothing much to do. There'd be payback sometime in the future, I was certain, but the expression on Kimberly's face at that moment was worth it. Her pinched-up mouth reminded me of Mr Cuddles's bum. Without another word, she stalked away.

Hep flashed me a tiny smile. 'Told you he's all right,' she whispered. In a louder voice she said, 'I need to talk to the band. If they don't play my favourite song next, things are going to get seriously ugly.'

She melted into the crowd, leaving me alone with a boy who made the object of my previous crush look like Ron Weasley. My stomach squirmed with a thousand ghostly butterflies.

'So,' I said, for lack of anything clever to say. At least the movie-me wouldn't have that problem.

'So,' Ryan agreed. 'How are you coping with the whole death thing?'

I considered the question. It wasn't half bad these days, since Jeremy had come along and we'd found there were other ghosts. 'It's OK. Jeremy helps.'

He tilted his head to one side. 'Jeremy?'

Ah. How to explain that one? 'My not-dead friend. Don't ask me why, but he can see me.'

Ryan looked intrigued. 'That must be useful.'

There was that word again – useful. Hadn't Hep said the same thing? 'Er, yeah. I suppose so.' I thought back to earlier that evening. 'Mostly he's just annoying.'

'What did you do before you died?'

Another good question. 'The usual stuff. Went to school, hung out with my mates. Played bass guitar in a rock band.'

'Really?' His eyes gleamed with interest.

'No,' I sighed. 'But I wish I had.'

'I know what you mean. I always wanted to play the Polynesian nose flute.' He shook his head tragically. 'I feel my life was incomplete.'

I grinned, pleased he knew how to play the game. 'Well, it just so happens that I'm very accomplished on the nose flute. I can teach you.'

His sapphire eyes twinkled. 'Lucky me. Actually, I play a mean bass guitar so I can teach you. When do you want to start?'

'Since I don't have a nose flute on me and you don't have a guitar it could be tricky. Unless you play air guitar?'

'I do, but there's a few things we need to get straight first. Best movie of all time?'

I didn't hesitate. '*The Goonies.*'

His eyebrows furrowed. 'Uh-huh. Favourite band?'

Uh-oh. This was where it could all go down the drain. Get it wrong and I might never recover my credibility. On the other hand, if I lied I'd be stuck with it for all eternity.

It was a tough call.

In the end I plumped for honesty. 'I'd have to go for Muse.'

With no indication of whether this was a good or bad thing, he nodded. 'Favourite song?'

Argh. Enough with the difficult questions. 'Erm . . . it depends on my mood, but usually I'd say "Unintended".'

'From the "Showbiz" album?'

I almost sagged with relief. Musical incompatibility was a deal-breaker. What if he was into frothy pop? I'd never be able to take him seriously. 'You like Muse too?'

'Nope. Give me a bit of R'n'B any day.'

I swallowed my disappointment. It was probably a good thing he had some faults. Besides, it meant I could teach him the error of his ways. I mean, seriously. *R'n'B?*

A vaguely familiar teenager appeared beside us. 'Sorry dude, we need you on the stage now.'

Ryan touched the other boy's fist with his own, then fixed me with a stern look. 'This conversation is not over. Wait here and do not move. I'll be back in a few minutes.'

Purposefully, he cut through the crowd. I hung around, trying not to look like a Billy No-Mates. It was too much to hope that Hep was nearby. I'd just have to wait and hope Ryan didn't forget about me.

When the opening notes of 'Unintended' floated up into the night air, I assumed he'd asked the band to play it for me. A warm glow bubbled up inside me. He'd requested my favourite song, even though he hated it; definitely a good sign. As the lead singer sang the first words I pushed forwards for a better view. It was amazing how different songs changed his voice. If I didn't know better, I'd say it wasn't the same person singing . . .

Realisation hit me. The band wasn't playing. Ryan was, and he was singing to me. Shock stopped me in my tracks and, as I listened, the familiar lyrics took on new meanings. A slow smile crept across my face. He focused on me, weaving a world containing only the two of us and the song. It was the most magical thing I've ever heard. I never wanted it to end.

The last strains died away. For a nanosecond the air was filled with absolute silence. Then the spell broke and the room erupted into cheers. Ryan was smiling, but didn't break eye contact with me. In that exact moment I knew two things: one, I'd met my soulmate and two, the timing sucked. Why couldn't we have met before we died?

Chapter 9

Every now and then there comes an experience which rocks your world so much that you remember it forever. In my case, forever really was an eternity, but I knew time would never tarnish the way I felt at that moment.

'Well? Did I get the job?' Ryan was grinning from ear to ear as he walked towards me.

I was far too busy fighting the goofy smile threatening to take over my face. 'What job?'

'Teaching you guitar.'

I gave in and let the smile win. 'Well, there were a lot of other applicants, but I took pity on you.'

'Did you like the song?'

Like it? That was was up there for understatement of the year, but I wasn't about to tell him that. Instead, I put on a sorrowful expression. 'You lied to me.'

He spread his hands. 'I'm sorry. It was worth it to see your face, though.'

Sniffing, I said, 'You'll be telling me next you lied about the nose flute.' I shook my head sadly. 'I've gone right off you now.'

His face split into a dazzling smile. 'Now who's lying? You're mad about me, I can tell.'

I laughed. 'Mr Confident, aren't you?'

'Always.' He raised an eyebrow smoothly. I tucked it away as another fact I liked about him. Maybe he'd even teach me how to do it.

'There you are.' Kimberly strutted over. Ignoring me completely, she pouted at Ryan. 'I've been looking for you everywhere.'

'He's been on stage,' I supplied helpfully. 'I'm surprised you didn't see him.'

She pretended not to hear. 'You promised me a dance.'

'I hadn't forgotten.' Ryan's tone was polite, but I could sense an edge to it. 'I'm busy right now.'

Kimberly let out a tinkling laugh. 'Surely you've done enough charity work for one night?'

I frowned. What was that supposed to mean?

'Shut up, Kimberly.' He was beginning to look angry.

'Haven't you told her?' Kimberly threw a pitying glance. 'I suppose you think he's been talking to you because he likes you.'

I eyed her uneasily. 'Maybe he does. Not everyone has

the personality of a pit-bull.'

An evil smile played around her lips. 'Ryan spends his time helping the newly dead to adjust.' Triumphantly, she went on, 'He's not speaking to you because he wants to, he just feels sorry for you. It's practically his job to waste time on losers like you.'

A roaring sound started in my ears. It couldn't be true. I'd felt a connection; we both had, I was sure of it. I turned to Ryan. His eyes were apologetic.

'Lucy!' A voice bellowed across the air.

Almost as one, the entire room stopped chatting and dancing and looked at Jeremy as he strode towards me. I stared in dull disbelief. Could things get any worse?

'Oh, for pity's sake,' I muttered, a deep scowl creasing my forehead.

Oblivious to the interested gaze of the surrounding ghosts, Jeremy called crossly, 'The last bus goes in ten minutes. We have to go now.'

Ryan threw me a sympathetic look. 'Let me guess. Your non-dead friend?'

There was no point in denying it. 'Yeah. Although he's going to be one of us very soon because I'm about to kill him.'

A low muttering had broken out. Clearly the other ghosts were working out that Jeremy was different and that he could see me. Curious glances were being tossed in my direction.

Kimberly got there quicker than most. 'You've got a pet

psychic? You really are a freak, aren't you?'

Maybe I should have come up with a cutting reply, but I had no answer. None of the other ghosts I'd met had someone like Jeremy. Maybe she was right – I was a freak.

Sensing she had me down, Kimberly went for the kill. 'Let me help.' She leaned forwards and grabbed hold of my plug necklace. 'You heard the man. It's time you went home.'

With a vicious twist, she tugged on the thin chain. It sank into my neck, causing a moment's fleeting discomfort. Then it snapped and she pulled her hand away, still gripping the plug. For a split second, nothing happened. Almost in slow motion, I saw Hep pushing her way towards me. A wave of dizziness washed over me and my ears clanged. Tiny black and white dots clouded my vision, like they had when I'd fainted in assembly. It felt like I was disintegrating where I stood. I fought to stay upright, but it was useless; I was being sucked away. Helplessly, my shocked eyes searched for Ryan. The last thing I saw before being dragged backwards was his sorrowful face.

'How bad was it?'

Jeremy hovered at the bottom of the stairs, his face etched with uncertainty. Sat on the only clean patch of floor, I turned my face towards the wall wordlessly. What sort of question was it, anyway? Less than an hour before, I'd been dragged, kicking and screaming, through half the buildings in the city. It felt as though my every molecule had been flipped inside out and jumbled back together any old how. How did he expect me to feel?

'Go away.'

He crossed the tiled floor to squat beside me. 'If it's any consolation, your friend landed Kimberly a serious wallop for what she did. If she wasn't a ghost, she'd be wearing a shiny black eye by now.'

The thought of Hep launching herself at Princess Perfect cheered me up a bit. I hadn't checked my phone. There was probably a gleeful text waiting for me. 'Remind me to thank her next time I see her.'

Encouraged by my response, Jeremy went on. 'The boy you were talking to gave her hell, too.'

I closed my eyes. I'd been trying not to think about Ryan. We'd hit it off so well; he couldn't have just felt sorry for me. Embarrassment rose up in a hot wave. I couldn't fool myself. There'd been truth in Kimberly's words, it had been written all over Ryan's face. And now that I knew I'd only been a pity case, I'd never be able to look him in the eye again. My own eyes snapped open. Wait one second . . . how on earth could Jeremy have known what happened after I headed off to the party?

'Before you ask, no, I didn't see any other ghosts. I met one of the psychics from the Dearly Departed as I left the party and she told me. Apparently, one of them goes along to these events to help set up and make sure no one else living goes poking around.'

I hadn't noticed any other living people there, but I'd

been blinkered by the love goggles. A giant pineapple could have been dancing the night away and I wouldn't have seen it.

'It was horrible, since you ask. I think I threw up.'

Crossing to where I sat, Jeremy squatted beside me. 'Are you up to a visitor? The psychic from the church said someone wanted to tag along and see you.'

A reluctant smile tugged at my mouth. 'Hep?'

He shrugged. 'Don't ask me. As far as I'm concerned there's no one up there except the homeless guy who sleeps in the doorway of the Tommy Hilfiger shop.'

It had to be Hep. I didn't really know any other ghosts. 'Send her down, then. I'd go myself, but the floor sways when I stand up.'

Minutes later, he was back with my visitor in tow. Surprise, surprise, it wasn't Hepzibah. I groaned silently. As if my night hadn't been humiliating enough, I had to face the last person I wanted to see my unglamorous home; Ryan was following Jeremy down the stairs to my dimly lit lair. Jeremy hovered by the steps, unsure what to do.

'Hi.' Ryan's voice echoed softly around the tiled walls as he neared me. 'How are you doing?'

I raised my shoulders listlessly. 'I've been better.'

He looked down at his trainers. 'I'm sorry about Kimberly. I don't know why she did what she did.'

Oh *please*. A five-year-old could figure out what Kimberly's problem was. I opened my mouth to tell him so. He beat me to it. 'Actually, I do. I've known for a while she was . . . er . . . interested in me. I suppose she saw how well we were getting on this evening and got jealous.'

'It doesn't make it OK.'

He sighed. 'No, but try not to be too hard on her. She's got problems.'

I stared at him incredulously. Kimberly had done what had to be the worst thing one ghost can do to another, and he expected me to cut her some slack because she had *problems*?

'Here's some breaking news, Ryan. We're stuck in spiritual limbo here. We all have problems.'

His blue eyes met mine. 'I know. That's what I do – try to help ghosts solve some of them. I'm not bad at it.'

'What are you, some kind of unofficial celestial social worker?'

He smiled. 'Kind of. I welcome the newly dead and help them pass on any messages to the living. The goal is to get them to move on, make them realise they don't have to stick around.'

I frowned. There were questions I wanted to ask, but they'd have to wait. 'Do the world a favour – move Kimberly on faster.'

'Deal.' His mischievous expression dissolved as he fixed me with a serious look. 'She was wrong, anyway. I wasn't talking to you because I felt sorry for you or because I had to.'

Jeremy cleared his throat uncomfortably. 'Are you going to be all right, Lucy? I wouldn't mind getting some sleep.'

Eek, I'd almost forgotten he was there. It had to be weird for him, watching me have a one-sided conversation with thin air, but then strange had become an everyday thing for Jeremy since he'd met me. I was just glad I hadn't said anything embarrassing. 'I'll be fine. Thanks for coming to check on me.'

Nodding, he said, 'I'll drop in tomorrow.' His gaze darted around the room. 'Bye, Ryan. Nice to . . . er . . . meet you.'

'Good to meet you too.'

'He said your trousers are too short,' I supplied.

Startled, Jeremy looked down. 'Really?'

'No,' I grinned. 'Go home.'

And then it was just the two of us. Ryan settled down on the floor next to me and didn't even flinch at the puddles.

'Welcome to my place,' I said to fill the silence, waving an arm around. 'Do you like what I've done with it?'

'At least you've got a roof over your head,' he replied, taking in the view. 'Actually, it's not that different from mine. Same smell, but there's no way to flush.'

I didn't answer immediately, unsure how to phrase the question I wanted to ask. It reminded me of the first time I'd gone swimming without my mum. I hadn't been sure of the best way to get into the pool; the steps were for babies. Eventually, I'd decided to plunge in at the deep end. 'Hep said you died in a car crash. Are you a homeless ghost, then?'

He grinned. 'Kind of. My dad and I crashed on the dual carriageway, so I don't have a building to haunt like you, but

I'm tied to the place all the same. You might have seen the flowers when you came to the party.'

'What happened to your dad?'

The grin faded. 'He's been in a coma since the accident. I don't see him much.' A melancholy expression crossed his face. 'I miss him. He was the one who taught me to play guitar.'

He looked so vulnerable, I wanted to reach out and touch him. 'He did a great job.'

Ryan nodded absently. 'My mum spends most of her time at the hospital, hoping he'll get better. Meanwhile, he's stuck in an even worse situation than us. I wish there was something I could do. At least if he was a ghost I could help him move on.'

I hadn't realised there was anything worse than being dead. My throat ached with sympathy. As well as being the most gorgeous ghost ever to walk the earth, Ryan was a genuinely nice person. I wanted to hug him. Actually, I wanted to snog his face off, but that was going to have to wait. Right now, it was enough to sit and talk.

'What about you? When are you going to move on?'

'I suppose I'll know when the time is right.' He scuffed one worn trainer against the other. 'In the meantime, we have some unfinished business. Usually, I know as soon as I meet someone. You're different.'

My stomach flipped. 'What do you mean?'

He studied me soberly for a moment, then shook his head. 'Nope, you'll have to put me out of my misery.' He tilted his face to one side. 'Marmite. Love it or hate it?'

I laughed out loud. 'Love it, of course.'

He looked delighted. 'Excellent news. I couldn't go out with a girl who didn't like Marmite.'

Oh flippity-flip, now my stomach was doing a full Olympic gymnastic routine. Had he really said what I thought he had? 'You haven't asked me yet.'

Blue eyes darkening as they met mine, Ryan nodded. 'I'm getting to that part. Lucy, will you go out with me?'

I thought about what my mates would say if they could see me now. Yuk, probably. But they'd also be advising me to play it cool, be an ice princess and make him wait. I looked at his tanned face, remembering how I'd felt when he'd sung to me earlier. He was one in a million. There was no way I was letting him get away.

'You'd have to promise never to play R'n'B in my presence.'

He held up a hand. 'Scout's honour. You do know I was kidding about that?'

I hadn't. The nose flute had been an obvious joke, but plenty of guys had been into dubious music at school. It was a massive relief that Ryan wasn't like them.

'Correct answer,' I said cheerfully. 'Congratulations. You've just won tonight's star prize – a date with Lucy Shaw.'

'Great.' He smiled back at me. 'Deciding to throw that party was the best decision I ever made.'

After he'd gone, I considered the evening. Getting sucked back to the toilet was something I never wanted to experience again, and I made a mental note to make sure I spent at least a few hours at home every day. I prodded my feelings some more. In spite of being stuck underground with only a dripping tap for company, I was the happiest I'd been for ages. Picturing Ryan's gorgeously dimpled smile, a grin of pure pleasure crept over my face. The afterlife had just got a whole lot more interesting.

Chapter 10

'We need to talk,' Jeremy announced as he delivered a fresh batch of reading material a few days after the party.

I didn't look at him. Ryan had suggested we go to the cinema, and I was scanning the local paper trying to find the perfect date film. It was harder than I thought.

'I've been doing some research, and I think I've discovered something about your murderer.'

My head jerked up, a sick feeling washing over me. 'What?'

'After I spoke to the psychic from the Dearly Departed, I spent a few hours surfing the internet looking for clues. I found some disturbing things.' His eyes rested seriously on my face. 'I don't think you were his first victim. There are others. I think he's tried it before.'

I shivered. Jeremy kept harping on about helping me to cross over, but if it meant reliving the dark night of my murder over and over again, I wasn't sure I was ready. Besides, things were pretty rosy in my garden at the moment. It wasn't perfect but, after a blissful first date at the Science Museum with Ryan, it felt as though things were just starting to go right for me again. As much as I hated living in a toilet, I didn't want to move on if it meant I lost the new friends I'd gained.

'Maybe we shouldn't start this.' I knew it wasn't what Jeremy wanted to hear. 'If the police couldn't catch my killer what chance do we have? I don't know if I even remember what he looked like.'

Jeremy seemed to have been expecting my reluctance. 'It isn't going to be easy, but what choice do we have?' His face softened. 'You can't hang around here forever.'

How could I explain that I wasn't sure I wanted to go? All Jeremy saw was what I'd lost by dying. He didn't understand that this shadowy existence was better than none at all, that maybe I'd found something I wouldn't have had otherwise. I seized at the nearest excuse to put him off. 'I don't have time for this now – Ryan will be here soon.'

Eyes resting on mine, he wasn't letting it go. 'Maybe if you could give me a few details, they might help me to join up the dots?'

I didn't want to. The part of me which had helped me cope with the aching loss of my family was telling me to leave the past alone. Something in Jeremy's insistent gaze, though, wouldn't allow me to run away. Reluctantly, I forced myself to remember.

'I was on my way home from a really crappy party, about eleven-thirty. My best mate was supposed to come with me, but she'd got stupid chickenpox and couldn't go, so like an idiot, I went on my own. Anyway, the party sucked and I decided to cut my losses. I promised my dad I'd get a taxi home, but it was a really long wait so I thought I'd walk.' My voice cracked to barely a whisper as the memories started to flow. 'The streets were quiet. Everyone was still partying, I guess.'

Jeremy nodded encouragingly. 'Then what happened?'

My chest heaved and I could almost taste the fear again. 'I could see someone watching me all the way along Carnaby Street. When I reached the loos he called out to me. He said he'd heard an animal crying in the toilet and thought some boys had been tormenting a puppy down there. He asked if I'd go down and check on it while he called the RSPCA.' Even in the depths of my worst nightmare, I managed a half-hearted snort. 'Like anyone would be dumb enough to fall for that. Anyway, he must have seen me turning away, because the next thing I knew, he'd hooked an arm around my throat and whispered that he had a knife. Once he'd dragged me down the stairs there was nothing I could do.' I lowered my head into my hands, misery pooling in my stomach. 'I couldn't get away, and it hurt so much.'

Jeremy's expression was wretched as he watched me

struggle not to cry. 'It's OK. That's enough for now.' He fiddled with his jacket while I composed myself. 'I'm going to keep digging, see what I can find out.' He stared at me, serious and worried-looking. 'We could be dealing with a serial killer. If I'm right, this man probably plans to kill again.'

The words dragged me down after he'd gone. Apart from the details I'd shared, I'd purposefully blocked out most of what happened the night I died. There'd been no point in going over it again and again on my own. But if my killer was out there deciding on his next victim, could I really sit back and let it happen? Didn't I have a duty to put a stop to his murderous ways? I forced the thought to the back of my mind. Finding him could cost me my new-found happiness. It wasn't a chance I wanted to take.

'Hep, can I ask you something?'

We were sitting on her old bedroom floor, practising flicking the Blu-tack from her posters at the wastepaper bin. So far, she was winning, but my aim was improving.

'Depends on the question.'

I tossed my gaze skywards. She could be so moody sometimes. 'Have you ever kissed another ghost?'

Her shot pinged off the window. She turned to stare at me. 'No. Don't you think I've got enough issues without adding romantic angst into the mix?'

She had a point. 'Suppose so. If you were going to, though, how would you do it?'

'Let me guess. We're talking about Ryan the Love God here, right?'

Move over Einstein, there's a new genius in town. 'I wasn't thinking of Gawjus George,' I said, referring to the dribbling old ghost who had taken a bit of a shine to me over at the Dearly D.

She shrugged and resumed her flicking. 'I suppose it's possible. It's only physical objects we have trouble touching, not ghostly ones. I'm not sure how satisfying a snog-fest would be, though. It can't be the same can it, without real lips?'

It had me worried too. After my trip to the cinema with Ryan, I'd had the distinct impression that we both wanted to take things a step further, but neither of us knew how. It was hard enough working out the right time to kiss someone for the first time without all the added complications of being dead. In the end, we'd settled for some deeply unsatisfactory arm touching and smiling at each other wistfully. Then he'd watched as I'd made my solitary way down the steps to my loo. It had to be up there as one of the most disappointing ends to a date in the history of the universe.

We played in silence for a minute. I was catching up. 'Won't your parents wonder where all the mess came from?'

'Nah. They're used to much worse things.' A sad smile crept over her face. 'Not long after I died, I emptied every box of cereal over the living-room carpet. Have you ever tried to get Sugar Puffs out of a faux-fur rug?'

Sometimes I didn't understand her. 'Why would you do that?'

She shrugged. 'I was angry and wanted them to know about it. They never understood why I committed suicide.'

I couldn't help feeling confused. 'And you thought you could communicate that best using cereal?'

'I was angry,' she repeated. 'I didn't say I was rational.'

'Did it help them get why you killed yourself?'

She flicked too hard. The ball bounced off the rim of the bin and stuck to the lead singer's nose. 'No. They couldn't work me out when I was alive. Why would they understand me any better now I'm dead?'

The force of her next throw made the bin rattle against the wall. Maybe I should have let the conversation go, but I could feel the strength of her feelings and hearing about some of Ryan's experiences had made me want to help. 'Did you write a suicide note?'

She stopped throwing and looked at me, eyes suddenly filled with tears. 'I tried. I lost count of how many times I started to write something that would explain why I was tearing their lives apart. I couldn't do it. Nothing I could say would help them understand the torture I went through every day at school. It even followed me home. Towards the end, I couldn't even escape online. My parents had no idea what it was like. How could they? Death was the only way out.'

I swallowed hard. It was difficult to imagine a life so unbearable that dying was a blessed relief. 'My school had an assembly. Did yours?'

She sniffed. 'Oh yeah. And all the bullies said they were sorry. Like I cared how they felt. They were only part of the problem.'

I began to understand. 'Do you think your parents will ever get why you did it?'

The light fitting above our heads began to sway gently as Hep vented her unhappiness. 'I want them to,' she whispered. 'But they'll never make the leap. It's easier to ignore me than make things right.'

We sat in miserable silence.

'I'm sorry,' I croaked after a few minutes. 'I had no idea.'

'Don't worry about it. Sometimes it helps to talk about it.' She sighed heavily and waved a hand towards the bin. 'It's your go. Don't think I've forgotten the score.'

I took careful aim, concentrating on forcing my emotions into a single, sharp burst. 'Hey, it was worth a try.' The shot spun out of control and landed a long way from the target. 'I'm not going to beat you in a fair fight. What's a little cheating between mates?'

Two days later, the weirdest thing happened. OK, so you could argue that my existence was filled with strange happenings. But this was peculiar even by my standards.

It was late evening. I'd been wandering around Covent Garden with Ryan, trying to pluck up courage to take his hand. My nerve had failed a couple of times, but I was determined to have done it by the time we got back to Carnaby Street. If it went well, I decided tonight was the night I went in for the kiss.

Just as I was about to make a grab for his fingers, Ryan raised his arm to point along the street. 'Isn't that Jeremy?'

Great. I couldn't exactly blame him, but Jeremy wasn't being a massive help in my relationship with Ryan. If he was heading to my toilets, he'd be seriously cramping my style. 'So it is. He must have just finished at the theatre.'

Ryan smiled. 'Let's go and say hi.'

What could I do? The two men in my life were spending half their lives hanging around public toilets for my benefit. It would be rude of me to ignore one in favour of the other. With a silent sigh, I trailed after Ryan. Almost immediately, I came to an abrupt halt. I'd recognise that shade of hair anywhere. The woman who'd walked in front of me was Elvira. The question was, why was she following Jeremy home from work?

'Ryan, slow down,' I muttered, remembering only too well what had happened the last time I'd shouted around Elvira. 'Wait!'

Ryan stopped and turned back to me. 'What's up?'

'Shh!' I had no way of knowing whether Elvira could hear all ghosts or only me. 'That's the woman I told you about from the theatre. The one with the cat, remember?'

He did. 'I recognise her. She came to the Dearly D once and tried to persuade the psychics to let a TV crew film there. What's she doing here?'

'Following Jeremy.' I shook my head, unease crawling through me. 'I've got a bad feeling about this. We'd better warn him before he does anything stupid.'

Elvira had obviously seen him head down into the toilets. She was peering down the stairs, craning her neck to see better and getting a few odd looks from the people passing by. We crept past her and headed down to meet Jeremy.

He smiled when he saw me. 'Hi. Been out?'

Ordinarily, this would have earned him a sarcastic remark for stating the obvious. I was way too worried for that. In silence, I put one finger to my lips. 'Elvira is waiting for you outside,' I whispered. 'I think she's tailing you. Has she said anything about me lately?'

Jeremy shook his head. Ryan climbed halfway up the stairs to see if she was still there.

'She's gone,' he said as he came back down.

Jeremy looked mystified. 'What on earth would she be doing here?'

It was obvious, at least to me. 'She suspects you of hanging about with ghosts and wants to find out more.'

Worried, Jeremy said, 'In that case, I'd better keep away for a while. If she sees me in here too often she'll know something is up.'

I tried to hide a triumphant little grin. I was so grateful to Jeremy and liked having him around some of the time, but he was becoming a major gooseberry. A few days without him was exactly what I needed to get down to some serious lip action with Ryan.

Chapter 11

Unless you're dead or psychically gifted, you probably have no idea that Leicester Square is haunted by a flasher. I didn't know either, until I copped an unwanted eyeful as I walked past the enormous Odeon cinema. Grinning like a maniac, he ripped open his grimy beige overcoat in front of me, before speeding away across the square and repeating the process in front of someone else. My mouth dropped open in disgust.

'What's the matter?' Noticing I'd stopped, Jeremy turned to look at me.

I shuddered. 'Trust me, you don't want to know.' I jogged to catch up with him. 'Where are we going again?'

'St James's Park. I've arranged to meet someone there who might be able to help us.'

The knock-on effect of Jeremy keeping away from the toilets was that all our arrangements had developed a touch of James Bond. Don't take that to mean that we started crashing expensive cars or using ingenious little gadgets all the time. It only meant we were more careful about everything. Jeremy now wore a flashing hands-free earpiece whenever we were out and about, allowing him to look as though he was completely normal when he talked to me. At least, as normal as anyone ever looked babbling away to no one. I couldn't help thinking Jeremy was taking the secrecy thing a bit too far, though. Before I knew it, he'd be talking in code and calling me Moneypenny.

'Is it too much to ask who we're meeting?' I asked. If he told me I'd find out when we got there, I decided I might scream.

'Her name is Sarah. There are some striking similarities with your story. I think she might have been stabbed by the same man as you, but she got away.'

My eyes widened as the words sank in. I was stunned he'd arranged the meeting without asking me. 'And she agreed to meet you?'

He gave me a grim nod. 'She took some convincing. I don't think she'll be on her own.'

Part of me wanted to thump him. I'd made it clear I wasn't keen to find my killer, and he'd ignored me totally. But I also understood he was trying to help, and now that he'd found someone else the man had hurt, I could hardly refuse to get involved. My anger ebbed away. How much had he told this Sarah, anyway? Probably not everything. How would you even begin to start a conversation like that? *Hi, I'm someone you've never met and I talk to the ghost of a girl murdered by the same man who attacked you.* I didn't think so.

It was a fabulous day and St James's Park was looking good. I missed being alive most when the sun was shining; I'd have given up soap opera updates from Jeremy for a month to be able to feel the sun on my skin one more time.

'How are you going to know what she looks like?'

We were strolling along a gravel pathway through the flowerbeds. The scent of the roses reminded me of the memorial garden at school. There would be a plaque there bearing my name by now. I grimaced. Dogs probably weed on it.

He waved the newspaper he was carrying at me. 'I told her I'd be sitting on the bench beside the lake, reading yesterday's *Times*.'

I rolled my eyes. 'Don't tell me. The newspaper bit was your idea.'

His eyes wouldn't meet mine. 'Might have been.'

'What makes you think she's going to show up?'

He shrugged. 'She said she would. If she changes her mind then we'll have to go back to the drawing board.'

It was ten to twelve when we reached the lake, and Jeremy had arranged to meet Sarah at midday. I'd never admit it to Jeremy, but I was hoping this Sarah wouldn't show up. I sat fiddling with my mended necklace, another plug wedged firmly in my jeans pocket. It ruined the look of my outfit, but since the Kimberly incident I was taking no chances.

There was a family feeding the ducks not far from us. I watched as their chocolate-encrusted toddler tried to throw a handful of bread towards the water. A few bits of bread landed beside my foot. Without thinking, I kicked out at one of them, taking great satisfaction as it flew over the lake. I was getting really good at touching things. *Maybe I should challenge Hep to a game of footie*, I thought.

'Lucy!' Jeremy lowered the newspaper and hissed at me, but it was too late. The boy had seen the bread leap up into the air, apparently on its own. He stared at the ground where it had been, then looked at the empty space on the bench beside Jeremy, a deep frown creasing his tiny forehead. He toddled nearer and repeated the process.

His mother noticed. 'Harry! Come here, please!'

Harry showed no sign of giving up his investigation. Instead, he picked up another piece of bread from the ground nearby and studied it suspiciously.

'Your mum's calling you,' I mentioned, earning a black look from Jeremy.

Apparently realising there was nothing special about the bread, Harry dropped it on the floor and glanced around. His eyes came to rest directly on my face.

'Bogies!' he said, almost conversationally, and wandered away.

I'm sure I never behaved like that when I was three. Children's television has a lot to answer for.

'I think this might be her.' Jeremy had clearly forgotten about the earpiece because he spoke from the side of his mouth. I sighed and thanked my lucky stars the fate of the entire world didn't rest on his undercover abilities.

He was probably right. Walking apprehensively around the lake towards us was a young woman, older than me, but way too young to be looking as frail as she did. Beside her was an older man with white hair. The woman was darting anxious glances at the people around her, as though she didn't trust any of them. Sympathy softened the last of my anger. Perhaps she'd been luckier than me at escaping her attacker, but that didn't mean she'd got off lightly. She wore a long-sleeved jumper, even though it was a hot day. Did she have scars she needed to cover? Or were the worst ones in her head?

Her gaze came to rest on Jeremy and her pace quickened. Closing the paper, Jeremy stood up as she approached. 'Sarah?'

She nodded. 'This is my dad.'

Jeremy shook the man's hand. 'Pleased to meet you. Thanks for coming.' He cleared his throat nervously. 'Would you like to sit down?'

Oh nice one, I thought. If they all sat down it left no room for me. 'I'll just sit on the floor then, shall I?' I said in a loud voice. 'Don't mind me.'

Jeremy ignored my grumbling. 'Well, as I said on the phone, I'm investigating the murder of a teenage girl in London. Some aspects of the crime bear chilling similarities to your attack and I wondered if I could ask you a few questions about it.'

'You're not a journalist?' Sarah's dad asked, his voice gruff.

Shaking his head, Jeremy said, 'No. The girl who died was a friend. I want to know what happened to her.'

At first, Sarah was unwilling to say much. I could understand that. Talking about the attack meant thinking about it, and I avoided doing that whenever possible. It was only natural Sarah would do the same. Jeremy was patient, though, and gradually he eased the story out of her.

It had happened late one evening the previous November. Sarah had been on her way home from the pub where she worked as a barmaid and had cut across Hampstead Heath like she normally did. She hadn't got far when a man approached her. He'd told her he'd seen a car hit a puppy on the road behind them. The injured dog had limped off into some bushes near the toilets; would she wait there while he went for help, in case it came out?

Sarah had agreed. While she waited, she sent a text to her sister at home saying she'd be a bit late. Minutes later, she was being dragged backwards into the toilets, a rough hand clamped over her mouth. Worried when she didn't turn up, her dad had gone looking for her and had found her where she'd crawled, blood-soaked and barely alive, out on the heath. There had been no sign of her attacker. Afterwards, the only thing she'd been able to tell the police about the man was that he'd had a peculiar, raspy voice and had a tattoo of a snake showing above the collar of his coat.

Gravely, Jeremy thanked Sarah and her father, promising he'd be in touch if he had any news. I stayed silent all the way home, stomach churning with relived misery. The facts were horribly familiar. My attacker had baited his trap with a fictional wounded puppy and tried to lure me into a toilet by saying he'd heard it yelping. He *had* sounded weird, like he'd had a sore throat. I'd forgotten that. I didn't remember a tattoo on his neck, but the idea nagged at me. I pushed the thought away. It had been cold the night I died. Maybe he'd covered it with a scarf.

'Lucy?' Jeremy's voice was gentle once we were alone in the toilets. 'Was any of that helpful?'

Wordlessly, I shrugged. Helpful wasn't the phrase I would have chosen. It felt more like the cuts inflicted by the knife had been torn open again.

A concerned frown wrinkled his forehead. 'OK. I think it's safe to say we're dealing with the same person. I'll see what else I can find out.'

I couldn't answer. Jeremy was doing this for me, but he didn't have to face the memories I did. My eyes skittered away from him as I struggled for calm. It was no use. The walls of the toilet seemed oppressive and too close. In my mind, I could see the pool of blood which had seeped from my wounds as my vision dimmed and I sobbed my last few breaths on the floor by the cubicles. Suddenly, I couldn't bear to be down there any more.

'I have to get out of here.' I stumbled towards the stairs.

'Where are you going?' Jeremy started to follow me, then stopped.

I couldn't answer. All I knew was that I needed to be out in the sunlight. I couldn't hide away underground any longer.

Chapter 12

No prizes for guessing that I went to find Ryan. He was at the Dearly D, chatting to Bob, who'd been a Tom Jones impersonator at a nearby pub until his untimely death from a heart attack. Even the sight of his orange tan and big hair couldn't raise a smile from me. Ryan must have read in my face that something was wrong. He said goodbye to Bob and came over to where I waited. Stumbling a little over the words, I explained what had happened. He didn't hassle me for details.

'What you need is something to take your mind off things. Come on, there's something I've wanted to check out for ages.'

We made our way to Camden Town and wandered along the side streets, talking about the silliest things we could think of. He described the braces he'd worn until a few weeks before the crash, I told him about the time I'd managed to fall off my horse in slow motion during a riding lesson, finishing up in an undignified heap in front of the instructor. By the time we got to our destination, the memory of meeting Sarah had faded.

'I still can't believe you've brought me to the zoo,' I said as we slid through the ticket barriers. 'I haven't been here for years.'

Ryan smiled. 'I used to love seeing all the animals. Most of all, I wanted to get up close and personal with them, but there were always barriers in the way.'

I caught on. 'So you're planning on doing it now?' Thinking back to the way Lucifer had reacted, I wasn't sure it was a good idea. A freaked-out domestic cat was one thing – but a lion or tiger? Things could get very messy.

'I promise not to scare them. Let's go and try the meerkats first.'

The animals adapted to our presence better than I expected. Some of them were more relaxed than others. We didn't stay long in the big cat enclosure because they were clearly disturbed, but the otters didn't flicker an eyelid and the meerkats were great, popping up and down in a flurry of activity to see if we were still there. My favourite place was Moonlight World, a dimly lit series of underground rooms containing all kinds of nocturnal animals. The bats were fascinated by us, which I couldn't work out.

'Aren't they blind?' I asked as a large bat unhooked itself from a branch and swooped around me in a circle.

Ryan held up a hand, frowning in concentration to make his skin solidify. The bat landed on his outstretched fingers. 'No, that's a myth. These are fruit bats, and have good eyesight, but they use sound waves to travel in the dark. I'd say they have more idea than most animals that we're here.'

I watched the bat take off. 'How come you know so much about them?'

'I was going to be a vet. I suppose that's why I feel so comfortable here.'

I'd had no idea what job I wanted to do when I finished school, beyond the usual daydreams of marrying a super-rich celeb, which was looking unlikely now, and living a jet-set lifestyle. Art had been my favourite subject but, as the school careers advisor had pointed out, it wasn't a proper career.

It was nearly closing time and there were only a handful of people around. We could have stayed but it didn't seem right somehow, so we made our way out of the bats' glass-fronted enclosure and headed towards the exit. As we neared the heavy black doors, Ryan stopped.

'Lucy, wait. There's something else I want to try before we go.'

I paused, throwing him a questioning look. He beckoned me into a dark corner.

'I really like you, Lucy.'

Zoing! went my stomach, doing its weird somersault

thing again. It was turning into a regular event where Ryan was concerned. 'I . . . er . . . like you too.'

He licked his lips nervously. 'Good. That's good, because what I was wondering was – if you wanted to – maybe we could try . . . kissing?' His wide eyes found mine. 'But if you don't want to it's fine.'

My breath came in shallow gulps. 'OK.'

His face lit up. 'Really?'

I nodded. 'Have you done it before? As a ghost, I mean.'

'No. Have you?'

Oh yeah, I'd made a habit of jumping other ghosts in the months I'd been dead. I didn't say that, though. Instead, I thought back to my last snog attempt, with Dean Watson at the Year Ten Christmas party. It had been wet, mostly, and Pringles-flavoured but deliciously tingly at the same time. 'Do you think it'll feel the same?'

'Because we're ghosts, you mean?'

'Yeah.' I smiled wistfully. 'I can't help wishing we'd known each other when we were alive. I know we can still touch each other, but it doesn't feel like it did before I died. Do you know what I mean?'

'Yeah.' He thought for a moment. 'Maybe there's a way to make it feel the same.'

He held up a finger and made it solid. I caught on and raised my own finger to touch it. For the briefest second my skin tingled, as though we'd really connected, instead of the shadowy touch I usually felt. I blinked unsteadily and lowered my hand.

'Almost.' I swallowed, nervousness and happiness battling to make themselves felt. 'It's almost like being alive.'

Ryan's eyes were steady on mine. 'This is going to work,' he whispered. 'Ready?'

I nodded and closed my eyes. Pouring all my concentration into making my lips real, I tried not to let my nerves put me off. It wasn't easy. Usually I summoned up some anger to help me make contact with the real world, but anger wasn't one of the emotions swirling inside me now. But passion was – maybe I could use that. I seized on the feeling and felt my lips change. Millimetres away, I could feel Ryan doing the same. Slowly, I leaned towards him until my mouth brushed his. I pressed gently into him, parting my lips and then – oh bliss of all bliss – we were kissing! I was actually snogging the delicious Ryan, just like we would have done if fate had been kinder.

Seconds later, we broke apart, panting with the effort of taking solid form even for such a short period of time. When we'd got our breath back, Ryan was grinning. 'That was amazing.'

I couldn't help it. A matching smile broke out on my own face. 'Yeah, it wasn't bad. We could do it again sometime, if you like.'

He reached down and took my hand. 'I might just take you up on that offer, Lucy Shaw.'

We let the evening rush die down before heading home. I knew something was wrong the instant we turned into

Carnaby Street. Around the top of the stairs to my toilets hung a cluster of interested onlookers and several television cameras appeared to be pointing towards the entrance. An uneasy frown creased my forehead. It didn't take a boffin to work out something weird was going on. The question was what.

'I don't like this. Let's take a closer look,' I said.

We edged nearer. Halfway down the stairs stood a woman with a clipboard. She was arguing with a man in a dark suit.

'Look, this toilet is a site of suspected paranormal activity and I intend to catch it on film.'

'As a council employee, I can assure you, madam, that the only thing you'll catch on camera here is members of the public using the facilities and they won't be very happy about you filming them.'

'*The Ghost's the Host* is a very well-respected scientific television programme. We're not a peep show.'

The man folded his arms, jerking his head towards the film crew. 'I don't care. There's no way I'm letting you in with that lot. Apart from anything else, it's more than my job is worth.'

The argument went on for several minutes before the woman gave up and stamped back up to ground level. My eyes followed her as she crossed to the cameras, and I caught a glimpse of magenta hair. I scowled. It could only be Elvira.

'That woman is turning into a major pain in the arse,' I

complained, pointing her out to Ryan. 'I don't fancy hanging around here while they sort this out. Let's go and find Jeremy. If he's not at work yet he soon will be.'

Jeremy took the news grimly. '*The Ghost's the Host* is the show that filmed here. They didn't find any evidence of ghosts, but you'd never know that from the show they churned out.'

'It doesn't surprise me,' I said. 'From what I saw of it when I was alive, the whole programme was pretty pathetic.'

He threw a glum look around the lighting box. 'There's no way they'll get permission to film in your toilet, but it's going to cause us problems. I don't think it's a good idea to go back there tonight.'

I stared at the floor glumly. 'Where am I supposed to go? I can't stay away too long – I'm not risking getting dragged back there.'

'You'll be OK for a while yet,' Ryan said. 'I've known experienced ghosts stay away from their haunting zone for anything up to a day. It wore them out, though.'

Alarm shot through me. The last thing I needed was another side effect to leaving the toilet. 'What do you mean?'

'I mean that staying away for that long is tiring. You'd need to recharge your batteries there before you could leave again, but it doesn't mean you can't keep clear most of the time.'

Sniffing, I folded my arms. 'Even if you're right, I still don't have anywhere else to go. No offence, but I don't want to hang around your subway all night.'

'Can't you stay at Hep's?' Jeremy suggested.

I gave it some thought. 'I don't know. She's a bit edgy these days. I think she's depressed – even more than usual.'

He was silent for a moment. 'I suppose you could sleep at my flat.'

I looked at Jeremy in surprise. He'd never spoken much about where he lived. 'Have you got a plasma screen? And MTV?'

Ryan grinned. 'Way to get those priorities right, Lucy.'

Fixing me with a level look, Jeremy said, 'No, and it's probably a good thing or you'd take up residence in my living room.' He heaved a sigh. 'Go and find something to do for a few hours. When I'm done here, I'll take you home with me.'

I tried not to show it, but I was genuinely excited. I didn't imagine for one minute that Jeremy's flat was a palace, but it would have sofas and a television and the floor wouldn't be swimming in pee. At least I hoped it wouldn't. I might even be able to convince myself I could feel the softness of the carpet under my feet. Elvira had set out to trap me, but she'd ended up doing me a favour. Maybe I'd even catch up with the latest happenings in Albert Square. A tiny grin crossed my face. Even if I couldn't be there all the time, I was looking forward to the first of many cosy evenings over at Jeremy's.

Chapter 12a

I'm not superstitious. I don't have a problem with black cats
(unless their name is Lucifer) or an irrational fear of ladders,
but for some reason it bothered me that Jeremy's flat was
number thirteen.

'Didn't you think about it before you moved in?' I asked
him as he held open the door.

'I can't say I gave it much thought, and I haven't been
especially unlucky.' He shut the door behind me. 'Apart
from meeting you, obviously.'

'Charming.'

My sarcasm was half-hearted. I was much more interested in nosing around Jeremy's flat. It was surprisingly
stylish. No dated carpets and flowery wallpaper for this boy
– the floors had been stripped back to the original wooden

boards and the walls were pale. Best of all, fastened to a wall in the living room was a large flat-screen television. With a burst of concentration I snatched up the remote and sank into the leather sofa with a blissed-out expression on my face.

'Ooh, *Friends* repeat! Why didn't we think of doing this before?'

Jeremy poked his head around the door. 'Because I like having some kind of control over my life? We need to work some house rules, Lucy.'

Eyes glued to the screen, I nodded absently. 'OK.'

'No all-night TV fests.'

Boring, but I supposed he had a point. Given the amount of catching up I had to do, twenty-four seven television was on the cards, but he had to sleep sometime. 'Go on.'

'No walking through walls. Use the doors and never walk into a room without letting me know you're coming.'

I dragged my gaze away from the screen. 'Are you worried I'll catch you getting dressed? Don't worry, I've seen it all before. I have a little brother, remember? But if it really worries you, I could sing cheesy pop constantly. Then you'll always know where I am.'

'I've heard your voice. A simple call when you're coming in will do.'

'Fine. Anything else?'

He shook his head. 'That'll do for starters. I'm beginning to worry about this boy band fixation you have.'

Shuddering dramatically, I said, 'Pray to any God who'll

listen that you never find out the truth.' Firing a stern look his way, I went on, 'Anyway, you're a fine one to talk about musical taste. Is that a Barbra Streisand CD I see over there?'

A tinge of red crept into his cheeks. 'It's not mine.'

Pull the other one, mate. 'Of course it is. Are you sure you're not gay?'

'Positive. But if I change my mind, you'll be the first to know.'

With that, he took himself off to bed. I settled down on the sofa with my new friend, the remote control. Once again, I thanked my lucky stars Hep had shown me how to handle physical objects. Back-to back-episodes of every TV show I used to love? It wasn't heaven but, short of kissing Ryan, it was as close as I got.

When I woke up the next morning, Jeremy had hidden the remote.

'I'll find it,' I called over the noise of the shower. 'I'll use my special supernatural senses.'

'Have you got any supernatural senses?' he asked a few minutes later when he came into the living room, dabbing his head with a towel.

'Might have.' I tossed my long hair over my shoulder airily. 'Who knows what I'm capable of? I may have hidden depths.'

'See if you can put some of them to good use and work out a way to persuade Elvira you don't exist.'

I searched the room through narrowed eyes. 'I think

better when I'm watching TV.'

Jeremy snorted, unconvinced. 'Why don't you head over to the Dearly D? Hep might come up with an idea.'

If I knew Hep, she'd have all kinds of suggestions about how to get rid of the film crew. I wasn't sure if acting out another bloodbath in my toilets was a good idea, though.

'I could just text her,' I pointed out, peering under the sofa.

'Lucy . . .' he warned.

'Fine.' I snatched the remote from behind a cushion and bobbed my head vigorously. 'I'll go and find her. As soon as I've caught up on season five of this show.'

'What I don't understand is why Elvira's got it in for you.' Hep and I were at the deserted park near to the Dearly D, seeing who could push their swing the highest. 'Was she haunted as a child?'

It had been bothering me too, ever since our run-in at the theatre. For someone who claimed to be psychic, she didn't have much of an affinity with ghosts. 'I think she wants to be famous. Jeremy told me she used to be an actress. Maybe she thinks capturing me on camera will help her career.'

Hep's swing soared skywards. 'We could find out where she lives and make her life a living hell? I've always wanted to put my fist through a TV.'

Sometimes I forgot Hep's state of extreme anger. Tempting though the idea might have been, it was probably bad karma. I wasn't in a hurry to get to the next plane, but I did plan to get there eventually. In my imagination, it was an amazing place, with wall-to-wall television, gigantic bean-bags and as much Ben and Jerry's as I could eat. I wasn't about to risk my place there by terrorising the living, even if she deserved it.

A gang of hoodies was approaching the play area, swearing and shouting and generally being objectionable. I shifted uncomfortably, glad we were invisible.

'What we need is some kind of distraction,' I said, allowing my swing to slow down and stepping back. 'Something to take the heat off me.'

'Or someone who'll enjoy the attention.' Hep watched as one of the boys started kicking the swing and another two tried to wrench the roundabout out of the ground. 'I think I know just the person.'

'Who?' I asked warily.

Hep waited until the boy nearest to us was squarely in line with the swing, then let rip with an almighty kick at the rubber seat. It connected firmly with the back of his head. He flew forwards, scattering the rest of the posse and causing a whole cluster of swearing to fill the air. They scrambled to their feet, staring wildly around for a moment, then ran for it. Hep grunted in satisfaction, her internal thermometer temporarily lowered. 'Someone who loves being the centre of attention and is every bit as devious as Elvira.'

My eyes met Hep's. 'Kimberly.' The more I thought

about it, the more I smiled. 'Poor Elvira. She's got no idea what she's let herself in for.'

I could hardly blame Kimberly for being suspicious when we caught up with her at the entrance of the Dearly D that evening. Wouldn't you be, if your arch-enemies suggested you volunteer to throw your afterlife into turmoil for the sake of fifteen minutes of fame?

'So let me get this straight,' she said, looking from Hep, to Ryan, to me. 'You want me to turn myself into some kind of freak show to take the heat off you?'

I shook my head mournfully at the others. 'I told you she wouldn't be up for it. Not everyone can cope with the pressure of being a national television star.'

'You'll just have to put up with it, Lucy,' Hep sighed. 'I know it's a pain having Finlay West hanging on your every move, but there's nothing you can do. Or maybe someone else will be interested. Who's next on our list?'

It was all part of our carefully laid plan. Finlay West was the gorgeous presenter of *The Ghost's the Host*. I hadn't seen him hanging round the day before, but if they did get permission to film, it could only be a matter of time before he turned up. Hep was convinced Kimberly wouldn't pass up the chance to be the centre of Finlay's attention. I could practically hear the cogs whirring as she thought it over.

Ryan thought for a few seconds. 'Amanda Sawyer,' he said, referring to Kimberly's hated rival for the queen bee crown. 'I'm sure she'll want to help out, and I think I just saw her go in.'

The three of us turned to leave.

'Wait,' Kimberly said. 'Did I say I wouldn't do it?'

We exchanged long looks. 'I don't know,' I shook my head in doubt. 'The more I think about it, the more I think Amanda would be perfect.'

The suggestion that an opportunity to show off might be slipping away was enough to convince Kimberly. 'OK, I'm in. What do you want me to do?'

Chapter 14

There are a few things I don't mind about being dead. Sitting in the super-comfortable deluxe seats in the cinema for free is one, although it's no fun when the world's most enormous man unknowingly sits on you – oh, how we laughed about that one. Wandering about without a coat in the rain without fear of a soaking is another perk. On that wet afternoon, almost every other soul around me was huddled under an umbrella or turning up the collar of their jacket. I, on the other hand, could cheerfully splash through puddles without the fear of soggy feet or a dreaded frizz attack on my painstakingly straightened hair.

We were on our way back from St Mary's churchyard in Islington, after a check in at the toilet first. Ryan had told me Kimberly had died of a fatal reaction to a bee sting on a dare gone wrong in the very graveyard she was now buried in. It was a pleasant enough spot in the daytime, but I could imagine it got seriously creepy at night, exactly the kind of place a paranormal television show would go nuts for.

The idea behind Operation: Elvira was simple. Jeremy was going to go for a drink with Elvira and confide in her about a teenage ghost he was helping. He'd already quizzed her to see how much she knew about my murder and discovered she'd moved to London months after the crime. Since Elvira didn't know much about me other than my suspected home, we hoped she'd swallow everything Jeremy told her. Then he'd lead her to the grave, Kimberly would find a way of proving her existence and Elvira would rush back to inform the producer of *The Ghost's the Host*. Before we could say 'cheesy TV presenter', Finlay West would be oozing all over her like a melted Starburst. It was genius. If Elvira asked Jeremy about the toilet, he was under strict instructions to 'confess' he'd been meeting his boyfriend down there. It was the only part of the plan he didn't like.

'Can't I just tell her the toilets are on my way home and handy for when I need to go? It's actually the truth.'

I sighed as we joined the crowd waiting to cross Charing Cross Road. 'It doesn't explain why you spend anything up to a couple of hours down there.' He looked unconvinced so I went on. 'Put it this way. Do you think anyone is going to be asking more questions after you've dropped that little bombshell on them?'

He took my point. 'For the record, I'm not gay.'

A woman in front turned underneath her umbrella and tutted sympathetically. 'Denial isn't the answer, love. You'll feel much better once you come out.'

Jeremy compressed his mouth into a flat line and said nothing. Unable to help myself, I smirked all the way back to his flat.

After two days part-time exposure to my channel-hopping ways, interrupted only when I headed back to the toilet to recharge, Jeremy was keen to regain possession of the remote control. He arrived home after work to tell me Elvira had taken the bait. He hadn't stuck to the plan, though. He'd improvised.

'I offered to take her there tomorrow evening before work. She wanted to see if she could pick up Kimberly's vibes.'

Remembering her reaction to me, I had a momentary pang of guilt for Kimberly. Then I recalled what she'd done to me and decided she and Elvira deserved each other.

'You do realise you're going to have to invent a boyfriend now so she doesn't get suspicious? How about calling him Romeo?'

He shook his head. 'Not necessary. She didn't ask.'

I grinned. 'That's even worse, she was being polite. I think she'd already guessed.'

'Can I remind you that this is only a cover story?' Jeremy replied, sighing. 'I might have a lot of gay friends, but I *am* actually straight.'

'You don't have to keep telling me, I'm not the one who needs convincing. Let's hope Elvira doesn't tell the whole world you bat for the other team.'

I defy anyone not to have been tempted to follow Jeremy and Elvira when they went to Kimberly's grave. Not wanting to cause Jeremy to accidentally speak to me, I hung back. My faith in Kimberly to go through with the deal wasn't exactly unshakeable, either. Knowing Jeremy wouldn't be able to see her, I wanted to see what she got up to in front of Elvira.

I needn't have worried. Jeremy had kept the details sketchy when he'd spilled the beans, and it quickly became obvious Elvira wasn't getting any sense of Kimberly. Although she swore she could feel a presence, Elvira described her as being lonely and crying for her mummy. It was about as far from the truth as it was possible to get. Kimberly cottoned on fast, too. Once she'd spotted me, there was no holding her back.

'If this woman is psychic, I'm Queen Victoria.'

It wasn't fair, since Elvira had proved she could hear me, but I was hardly about to start defending her. I shrugged and decided to add a little atmosphere. 'Oooooooh . . .' I warbled in a suitably miserable tone.

Elvira's head snapped round. Encouraged, I figured I might as well practise my acting skills. 'Help meeeeeee.'

Jeremy did his valiant best to ignore me. 'You won't tell anyone about this, will you, Elvira?' he said in a reasonably convincing anxious voice. 'I don't want Kimberly to be disturbed. She's very sensitive.'

I bit my lip to prevent a snort of laughter escaping. Kimberly, sensitive? It was like describing cross-country as good, clean fun.

Elvira had her eyes closed and was swaying back and forth, presumably in an attempt to channel the spirit world. 'Hmm? Oh no, I won't tell a soul.'

'You're all tragic, you know that?' Kimberly shook her head. 'I can't believe I'm doing this.'

'The vicar's really nice,' Jeremy continued, throwing me a warning glance. 'I don't think he'd like hordes of ghost-hunters all over the place.'

We didn't meet the vicar, but it was probably true. If he had any sense, he'd charge the production company a small fortune for the privilege of filming and put the money and publicity to good use repairing the church.

Elvira's beady eyes were fixed on Kimberly's white marble headstone. 'Trust me, Jeremy. All your secrets are safe with me.'

Twenty-four hours later, all hell seemed to have broken loose at St Mary's. The woman with the clipboard I'd seen outside my toilet was back and arguing with the vicar. Camera crews were poised at the edge of the churchyard and Kimberly was psyching herself up to give the performance of her afterlife. Hep had come along to watch the fun.

'I think I'm going to come across as sad but plucky, with a hint of naughtiness,' I heard Kimberly boasting to her. 'I hope the people from my old school see it.'

Hep was moodier than ever. She seemed so deep in misery these days I was beginning to get seriously worried about her. Every time I tried to get her to talk about her unhappiness she went silent. It was something I planned to discuss with Ryan at the first opportunity. Maybe he knew a psychic psychotherapist or something.

In the meantime, the vicar had figured out he had an opportunity to pull in some money for the church roof fund. Clipboard Woman rolled into action, summoning in the crew and setting up cameras in every imaginable place.

'You will be respectful of the dead, won't you?' the vicar bleated in an anxious tone as a cameraman clambered on to a crumbling stone tomb.

'Of course we will,' the woman replied, her voice dripping with false sincerity. 'That's the whole point of the show, to let the departed get their message across.'

Ha, I thought with a cynical sniff. Actually, the point of the show seemed to be to exploit innocent ghosts who were just minding their own business. It just so happened that in this case it was a two-way street and the ghosts had some exploitation of their own planned.

At first, Kimberly didn't have much to do. After the cameras were set up, Finlay West arrived, along with the show's on-screen paranormal expert and a couple of Z-list celebrities who were trying to bump-start their dying showbiz careers. The crew took a couple of atmospheric shots around the churchyard before zooming in on

Kimberly's grave. Someone had done their homework because Finlay knew all about Kimberly, describing her as 'a beauty princess denied her chance to become a queen'. Hep and I almost spewed simultaneously at that point but, as you'd expect, Kimberly lapped it up.

Then they got down to the serious part of sensing the supernatural vibes. We watched with interest, safe in the knowledge that Kimberly hadn't done a thing yet and was sitting on the grass beside us, watching. An aging ex-boy band member swore he'd felt a ghostly breath blowing in his ear and the so-called psychic announced Kimberly's ghost was deeply disturbed. That bit was true, at least. She hadn't stopped ranting about the low quality of celeb they'd dug up.

'An ancient pop star and a couple of women who tell you how to clean your house? Is that really the best they could do?' She got up and walked across to the psychic. 'Boo!'

Coincidentally, the psychic did seem to react. His face crumpled into a sad expression. 'I can hear crying. She's telling me she didn't want to die so young.'

'Duh!' Hep said with a disgusted shake of her head. 'I can't believe people actually watch this crap.'

Kimberly approached the woman with the clipboard and gave the top of the board a deliberate tap. Forehead creasing into an absent frown, the woman's eyes stayed on the scene beside the grave. Kimberly tapped again. The frown deepened. Rolling her eyes with scorn-filled boredom, Kimberly smacked the board with such force it somersaulted high in the air and landed on a nearby gravestone with a loud clatter. The producer screamed.

'S-something jerked the clipboard out of my hands!' she stuttered, eyes wide. 'I felt it!'

There was no stopping Kimberly after that. The camera couldn't keep up with her as she moved around the churchyard, striking terror into the presenters and crew. Cameras teetered precariously on their stands, the sound guys had the microphones snatched from their hands and no sooner had the producer picked up her clipboard than it was sent spiralling upwards again. The presenters fled immediately and the crew weren't keen to hang around a moment longer than it took to gather up their gear before they ran for it. Even Elvira was spooked. I nearly felt sorry for them. Despite working on a paranormal TV show, it was probably the closest any of them had come to meeting a real ghost. Unluckily for them, she had an attitude the size of Africa.

I leaned back on the grass and reflected on the afternoon's work. Things had worked out perfectly. Now that Elvira's appetite for ghostly goings-on had been satisfied, she'd leave me alone, and Kimberly had got her fifteen minutes of fame. I couldn't wait to see the programme they cobbled together out of it all.

Chapter 15

Ryan poked his head around the top of the toilet stairs later that evening. 'All clear.'

The news gave me mixed feelings. On one hand it was a relief to know I could come and go from the toilet without worrying about being caught on hidden spook-cams. On the other, I'd got used to the comforts of Jeremy's flat and had formed a meaningful relationship with his remote control. I was going to miss it.

Sensing my reluctance, Ryan suggested we take a stroll along the South Bank of the Thames. We left Jeremy at the stage door of the theatre and chose a route which took us past Big Ben and across Westminster Bridge. Judging from the lack of coats on the people around us, the air was still warm. I wished I could feel it; cold I could live without, but the gentle embrace of the sun was something I missed. Lining both banks of the river were twinkling lights and reflected in the water was the glowing ring of the London Eye.

'Have you ever been on it?' I asked as we leaned on the stone bridge and gazed at the barely moving wheel.

'Yeah, my dad took me once.' He was quiet for a moment and I knew he was remembering. Then he flashed me an inviting grin. 'Fancy seeing the sights from the heights?'

The rhyme made me smile. 'I didn't know you were a poet.'

He winked. 'There's a lot you don't know about me. Come on, let's be proper tourists. We can sneak into one of the pods.'

If I thought London looked gorgeous from the ground, it looked even better from the air. Our capsule was jammed with clicking Japanese tourists, but it didn't matter. As we climbed into the night sky, I leaned back into Ryan's arms and soaked up the moment. I'd dreamed my whole life of meeting someone like him. I wasn't about to let the small matter of my death spoil it.

'What do you think it's like when you pass across?'

He thought for a minute. 'I don't know. It would be nice to think it's whatever you want it to be. Sometimes I get scared thinking about it, but I don't believe in the idea of heaven and hell.'

'You don't think we just stop existing then?'

I felt him shake his head. 'I think there's more to it than that. If there wasn't anything beyond this world, there wouldn't be anything such as ghosts and I'd have been wasting my time moving people on.'

He had a point. It did seem a bit odd to be striving to resolve whatever was tying you to the earth only to discover there was nothing worth trying for. Why bother? Being dead wasn't great, but it wasn't totally rubbish. I snuggled back against Ryan and gazed over the twilit city. 'I wonder how you know, when it's time to go.'

'Now who's being poetic?' he teased and I felt him smiling into my hair. 'I've seen it happen to other ghosts. They're surrounded by light and seem to become transparent. Some of them said they feel drawn to something they can't see. Then they gently fade away, but I don't think it feels bad.'

The idea filled me with quiet panic. I knew Jeremy wanted me to catch my killer and move on, and I understood he thought it was in my best interests, but I was scared. No one knew where you went. What if it was a dump? Or downright nasty? Plus, I wouldn't know anyone there. Did I want to go back to being lonely, without any of the friends I'd made? Most of all, could I bear to leave Ryan? It was all so unknown, and that was what scared me the most. I wasn't sure I was brave enough to take the chance.

Ryan picked up on my uncertainty and did his best to soothe me. 'Don't worry. We'll be going there together.'

I pulled away to study his face, biting my lip anxiously.

'How do you know?'

He smiled and lowered his lips to brush mine. 'Because it's fate. We're meant to be together, you and me. Nothing can separate us now.'

It didn't matter what Jeremy thought – his flat was always going to be the venue for our *The Ghost's the Host* viewing party. Kimberly's episode was being aired the following Sunday and, according to Jeremy, Elvira had been beside herself with excitement.

'It's ground-breaking television,' she'd told him the day after the graveyard filming. 'I wouldn't be surprised if we get international recognition from the paranormal community.'

Jeremy had voiced concern. 'It sounds to me like Kimberly is upset.'

Puffing out her cheeks in dismissive arrogance, Elvira brushed away his anxiety. 'She's undoubtedly a tormented spirit. I'm looking for a way to help her rest in peace.'

Kimberly certainly looked peaceful to me, leaning into Ryan on Jeremy's sofa. In fact, she had an air of the cat who'd got the cream. I had a feeling that if she could just get her claws into my boyfriend, her afterlife would be complete. Hep hadn't been happy about inviting her but, as I pointed out, without Kimberly it could be me making my presence felt on that TV screen. Unfortunately, I owed her. It wasn't a comfortable place to be.

The opening credits of the show began to roll and we settled down to watch. I had to admit the camerawork was slick. The churchyard looked like something out of a horror movie. Finlay West was grim-faced as he set the scene, drawing a picture of Kimberly as a sweet teenage girl, captain of the school netball team and loved by everyone. As one person, we turned disbelieving eyes on her. She gave a delicate shrug. 'The bit about the netball is true. We won the league two years in a row when I was captain.'

I bet they did. The opposition probably took one look at Kimberly's scowling face and ran away.

'Kimberly Jones had everything to live for,' Finlay finished off, gazing sorrowfully out of the TV. 'Maybe she has unfinished business. It's just possible we can help.'

Even though we never actually saw her on the screen, Kimberly obviously felt she was a TV natural. It was clear she loved the attention and considered herself the star of the show.

'My drama teacher always said I had presence,' she preened, as the pensioner pop star moaned that he'd felt someone push him.

By the end of the programme, I was beginning to wonder what we'd created. Kimberly had been a diva before she'd died and, now she'd got a taste of the limelight, I couldn't help wondering if she'd be gate-crashing other TV shows. Had we just unleashed the world's most demanding ghost on to an unsuspecting viewing public?

Finlay West appeared equally worried. 'It seems we've uncovered a hornet's nest of supernatural stress. Join us next week when we attempt to set Kimberly's soul to rest.'

Bursting with self-importance, the significance of that last sentence seemed to be completely lost on Kimberly. 'I'm going to be the talk of the school.' She flicked her hair, her expression smug. 'Again.'

'What did he mean by the part about setting your soul to rest?' I said slowly.

Kimberly ignored me. Throwing me a warning glare, Hep shook her head slightly.

Feeling stubborn, I refused to let it go. 'Jeremy? What does that mean?'

'I wondered that, too,' Jeremy admitted. 'Maybe I'll ask Elvira.'

'Whatever,' Kimberly sighed with an arrogant toss of her hair. 'I'm way too good for that bunch of losers.'

Eventually even my sainted boyfriend couldn't take any more of Kimberly's self-congratulation. 'The main thing is we got the result we wanted. Lucy can go home, and I think that's where I'm taking her right now.'

Kimberly pouted prettily and clutched his arm. 'She knows where she lives. I'm sure Jacob here recorded the show. I thought we could watch it again, just the two of us.'

Ryan's smile was tolerant. 'I'm sure *Jeremy* has other plans. Anyway, it's past my bedtime. My mother will kill me.'

She couldn't ignore the hint, but her spiteful glance at me once Ryan's back was turned said it all. She didn't like being in second place. Luckily, there wasn't a lot she could do about it.

Hep wasted no time putting me straight as we waited for the bus after dropping Kimberly off. 'What did you have to mention that bit at the end of the show for?'

I frowned. 'I have a bad feeling about it. Do they actually know how to put a ghost to rest? What if it goes wrong?'

'And that would be a problem why?'

'Hep, I know she's a cow, but we can't sit back and let something happen to her.' I gave her a meaningful look. 'We're dead. Haven't we been through enough? Even her.'

She wasn't convinced. 'I still don't know why you don't let her get what's coming to her. You need to watch it where she's concerned. She's got her sights set on Ryan, and I reckon whatever Kimberly wants, Kimberly gets.'

The words rattled around in my head a long time after we'd seen Hep home and Ryan had left me alone. Was I being too kind? I didn't think so. My existence was complicated enough without any extra guilt if something went wrong. If I could help Kimberly, I would. Ryan was too smart to get sucked in by her Little Miss Innocent act. Wasn't he?

Chapter 16

I was born on the sixth of December, which makes my star sign Sagittarius. On the day I died, my horoscope said I was supposed to *try your hardest to accept life's little ups and downs.* The joke wasn't lost on me in the months I spent afterwards loitering around the loo.

According to Minerva Mason, astrologer for one of the glossy magazines Jeremy brought me, my horoscope for September warned me that I might meet someone who was not what they appeared to be. I could have done with a bit more detail to be honest, but Minerva wasn't great on the finer points.

I didn't have a lot of time to dwell on it, though. Hot on the trail of my killer, Jeremy had been trawling through old newspaper records at the library with the kind of time and dedication the police hadn't been able to spare during their investigation. He chased down even the tiniest lead, dragging me reluctantly along behind him. If he showed me another picture of a tattoo I thought I might scream.

'I told you, I didn't definitely see anything on his neck. It was dark.'

'I know, but it might jog your memory. If we can work out what the tattoo was, maybe it'll help us find the man who killed you. Or at the very least I can take what we find to the police.'

'Like they'll be any help. You'd be better off showing it to the other girl he attacked. Sarah, wasn't it?'

He sighed. 'I don't want to upset her. She's been through a lot.' Realising what he'd said, he added hastily, 'Not that you haven't. It's just you seem a bit stronger, somehow.'

I knew what he meant. Sarah would spend the rest of her life looking over her shoulder, being afraid. In my case, the worst had already happened.

'I suppose it might help if she knew he was behind bars.' I bit back a sigh and nodded at the designs he'd picked up from the tattooist. 'Show me the pictures again.'

Hep refused point blank to get involved with helping Kimberly. 'She's evil and deserves everything she gets.'

It was a gorgeous day and we were sitting in Regent's Park, watching university students playing a game of rounders. After tennis, it had been the only sport to raise my enthusiasm at school.

'Jeremy spoke to Elvira. They've got some specialist in exorcism flying in from Romania and are planning to televise it live this Sunday night.'

Hep tugged at the grass moodily. 'So?'

'So we need to find a way to stop them.'

Predictably, Hep said, 'Why?'

There was a cheer as one of the boys smacked the ball solidly through the air. He didn't hang around, racing around the jumpers they were using as posts to make it home before the fielders had even retrieved the ball. I nodded approvingly. If I'd been captain, I'd have picked him over sporty Kimberly any day. 'Because no matter how horrible she is, I don't want to spend the rest of my eternity wondering if we made a mistake. Maybe the dead should stay out of the limelight.'

Another shout rang out across the park. I looked up to see the ball spinning through the air towards us.

'Catch!' The bowler bellowed to his fielders.

Without thinking it through, I rose and stretched my fingers skywards. My hand solidified at the exact moment the red sphere reached us and there was a satisfying smack as it hit my palm. For a second, I stood with the ball in my grasp and the elation of taking the catch ruled supreme. Then realisation hit and I froze. The fielder racing towards us skidded to a halt just centimetres away, staring in mesmerised astonishment at the ball, which apparently hung in mid-air. Tentatively, he held out a hand. I let go. The ball dropped into his waiting fingers. He gazed in wonderment at it before turning and waving it at his astonished friends. A ragged cheer went up.

Hep shook her head sarcastically as the students gathered around their friend. 'Nice one, Lucy. That's what I call lying low.'

By Sunday evening, I was as close to a nervous wreck as I'd ever been. Hep was still being dismissive, and Kimberly had decided I was envious. Jeremy had taken me seriously enough to read up on exorcism and shared my uneasy feeling that trouble was in store. No one had any suggestions about what we could do to stop it, but they convinced me it was pointless to try and talk Kimberly out of being at the cemetery when the cameras rolled again.

We got as close to the centre of the action as we could – no easy task with camera crews and burly bouncers everywhere. Since the show had aired the previous week, a lot of would-be ghost-hunters had turned up to watch the filming, and the bouncers were there to keep them away from the grave itself and whatever the show intended to do. None of the previous celebrities had wanted to take part again so there was a fresh crop of eager wannabes and has-beens hanging around, trying to look keen.

The Romanian paranormal expert called himself Dr Cristea and looked like he was auditioning for a horror film. He wore head-to-toe black and a seriously brooding expression. The overall effect was spoiled by the make-up girl dabbing foundation on to his face. Elvira was there, hovering around the edge of the filming area. She'd proved useful in getting Jeremy past the bouncers, but if she knew what was going to happen next, she was keeping her lips sealed.

The grave itself looked like it'd had a run-in with an occult fly tipper. Apart from the time I'd been dared by my mates to go into the incense-scented magic shop in Bluewater shopping centre, I'd never seen so many weird symbols and candles in lanterns.

'Over-accessorise much?' I said to Hep as we stared at the circle of signs. 'Any idea what it all means?'

She raised her shoulders nonchalantly. 'Trouble for Kimberly, I hope. Have you noticed how she's draping herself over Ryan?'

I glanced over. Kimberly had a possessive hand resting on Ryan's arm. Turning my back to them, I squinted at the markings on the ground. I knew Hep was trying to get me on her side, and I wasn't taking the bait. 'I think it might be a reversed pentagram in the middle there. That can't be good.'

'Depends on your point of view.' Her eyes narrowed suddenly. 'Shhh! Elvira's heading this way.'

'We should be ready to begin soon,' I heard Elvira's whiny voice say to Jeremy.

He shuffled uneasily. 'What actually happens?'

Elvira's expression became ghoulish. 'No one really knows. Exorcism is an ancient rite used on anything from ghosts to demons. The main thing is, they disappear.'

'What if they don't want to go?'

She laughed. It wasn't a pleasant sound. 'They don't have a choice. It's better for them in the long run than hanging around here, harassing the living.'

Jeremy watched her in silence for a moment. 'Why do you hate them so much?'

Her pierced lip curled into a bitter smile. 'You noticed? Since you ask, my mother was psychic, which meant I grew up being plagued by the dead.' A hunted expression crossed her face and she shuddered. 'I could never see them, but I heard enough of them. Sometimes they would scream all night. They terrified me. I promised myself that when I was older, I'd do everything in my power to get rid of them.'

'Did they ever do you any harm?' Jeremy asked softly.

Elvira scowled. 'That's not the point. This world is for the living. It's no place for the dead.'

She stamped away, leaving the three of us to stare in stunned silence at her retreating back.

'I'm sensing a bit of hostility there,' Hep said after a while, raising a thoughtful eyebrow.

I was wondering what exorcism was like. It had a demonic ring to it; what if it hurt? Maybe I needed to have one last quiet attempt at talking Kimberly out of taking part.

I might have known I was wasting my breath.

'You're jealous,' Kimberly accused, once I'd aired my concerns. 'You don't want me to be the centre of attention. Who believes in all this magical mumbo-jumbo, anyway?'

'She's not jealous, Kimberly,' Ryan said, frowning. 'You should listen to her. She might be right.'

Kimberly rolled her eyes. 'Not you as well. Trust me, it's all for the benefit of the cameras. They'll need more than a couple of candles to get rid of me.'

Needless to say, she was wrong.

Chapter 17

It's been said before that I don't know when to give up, but Kimberly's refusal to listen had even me beaten, and I could only stand and watch.

At first, it didn't seem like anything was going to happen. As the sun sank and the sky darkened, Dr Cristea began talking into the camera, his thick Romanian accent making even the most boring sentences sound creepy. Occasionally, Finlay asked a question. Each of the celebrities was sent to light the candles, which took longer than they expected, mostly because I followed them around blowing them out. Eventually, though, they were all lit and, once they were all stood in the middle of the circle, the chanting began. A deep sense of unease wormed its way through my stomach. The words weren't familiar. They didn't even seem to be

English, but they sounded like deeply bad news for any ghost, especially one whose grave stood in the centre of a pentagram.

Kimberly's attention was dragged away from Ryan. Frowning, she moved closer to the ring of candles. As her foot stepped over the line of the outer circle, everything changed. With a thin, high wail, Kimberly was dragged into the centre of the pentagram. Out of nowhere, a fierce wind sprang up and buffeted both us and the cameras. The volume of Dr Cristea's monotonous voice increased.

'It looks like we may have something.' Finlay directed his wide eyes to the camera. 'Hang on, things could get hairy.'

In slow motion, I turned to look at Kimberly. She was screaming in terror and struggling to free herself, as though something had hold of her ankles and was pulling her into the ground. Hep watched, her face expressionless, but Ryan looked shocked. Jeremy was staring at a gloating Elvira in bewilderment.

'Someone help me! Lucy, please, it's dragging me in!'

I stared wildly around. The trees were bending dangerously under the pressure of the wind, and leaves were being torn from their branches. Above the shriek of wind, I could hear the relentless voice of the exorcist. In the midst of the pentagram, Kimberly looked small and terrified, her shrill screams piercing the chaos around her. She seemed to be disintegrating before my eyes. I couldn't stand it any longer.

'No, Lucy!' Hep shouted as I moved past her, realising my intentions a fraction too late.

I stumbled forwards, ignoring her cry, and held out my hand to Kimberly.

A faint glitter of triumph flickered in her eyes as she latched a vice-like grip on to my wrist. 'That was really stupid, Lucy, even by your standards,' she hissed, and pulled me into the pentagram.

The instant I was inside, my legs turned to dead-weights. I glanced down to see my beloved Uggs were stretching and distorting as the spell sucked me in.

'Let go.' I tugged backwards. 'If I can reach the others maybe we can pull you free.'

Her pretty face twisted into a sneer. 'It's too late for that, you idiot. I can't get out. Still, every cloud has a silver lining.'

Fear clutched at my stomach. 'What do you mean?'

The hand on my wrist tightened. 'Can't you even figure that out? What the hell does Ryan see in you?' she spat. Around us, the howling wind intensified. 'You planned this, didn't you?'

Stunned, I shook my head. 'That's not true!'

'Don't deny it. You wanted me out of the way so you can have him all to yourself. Well, it's not going to happen like that.' Her lip curled in scorn. 'If I have to go, I'm taking you with me. Say goodbye to your precious Ryan!'

Below her, a gaping red slit was opening up. It didn't look inviting. In desperation, I tried to prise her fingers off me. It was no good – she wasn't letting me go. Thrashing in helpless panic, I missed Jeremy bellowing my name, didn't see him charging forward to grab hold of the plug chain around my neck. It was only when I felt the metal dig into me and the chain fall away that I realised what he was trying to do. With renewed urgency, I thrust my free hand into the pocket of my jeans and made a fist around the spare plug that nestled there. Praying to any god listening, I dragged my hand out. As Kimberly's face began to dissolve in front of me, I looked deep into her eyes. 'I don't think I'll come after all. Good luck, Kimberly.'

The crimson chasm was widening. I could feel it sucking us in. My vision started to turn salt and pepper. I didn't have long, seconds maybe. Summoning all of my strength, I hurled the plug as far away as I could. The second it left my fingers there was a terrible roaring in my ears. A nanosecond later I felt a bone-crunching lurch, as though my soul was being wrenched from my body. The world tilted and turned black. I let out a horror-filled, silent scream and collapsed into the pitch darkness.

'Lucy?'

I could hear the voice. It sounded very far away. Whoever it was should leave me alone. I couldn't remember ever feeling more wrecked.

'Lucy, wake up!'

My eyes snapped open. 'Go away, I'm tired.'

Jeremy's white face swam into view. 'Oh, thank goodness you're all right.'

It took a lot of effort to stay focused on his still-worried eyes. 'What happened?' I mumbled. 'Where's Ryan?'

Ryan appeared behind him. 'I'm here. We were at the churchyard with Kimberly, remember?'

My mind struggled over the words. We'd gone to watch the filming at Kimberly's grave. I'd been trying to warn her about something. I moved my head to look around. How did I get back to the toilet? A stab of fear clutched at my heart. What in the name of all that was holy had gone on?

'I remember it got very windy,' I said, my voice thick and slurred. 'And there were words, horrible words which didn't mean anything, except that they did. I don't understand. What happened?'

Ryan smiled down at me gently. 'It's not important right now. All that matters is that you're here and you're OK.'

Jeremy raised his head. 'She's confused. I don't think she should be alone. Ryan, I know you must be here. You and Hep can come back to the flat for a while. We can take it in turns to watch her.'

I tried to move my head to see Hep, but it was heavy and darkness was closing in. The last thing I felt before slipping into unconsciousness was Ryan's comforting arms sliding beneath me.

It was almost a week before I was back to full strength. Getting to and from the toilets was exhausting, but it had to be done. No one had seen anything of Kimberly. It didn't surprise me. I'd seen more than enough of the hell-hole she was headed for and it didn't look like the kind of place anyone came back from. Jeremy had recorded *The Ghost's the Host* for me. I plucked up the courage to watch it one afternoon with Ryan. It didn't look anything like as terrifying as it had been and there was no sign of either Kimberly or me on screen. Anyone watching at home would have had no idea that one ghost had been banished and another had barely escaped.

Jeremy reported that Elvira had been thrilled with how the exorcism had gone. Obviously, she'd had a better idea than anyone from the show about what had gone on. I was only grateful she hadn't heard Jeremy call my name as he'd dived forwards to save me. She thought he'd been trying to rescue Kimberly.

The incident made me even more apprehensive about passing across. What would it be like? Who even knew where you'd end up? But it did make me realise I didn't want to head to the next plane with any unfinished business on Earth. That probably meant finding my killer. I didn't share this revelation with Jeremy, although I did start to chip in during our frequent progress updates. Not that he needed my encouragement – he was a man on a mission.

If I thought the trauma of my narrow escape would earn me much down-time, I was wrong. He arrived at the toilet one afternoon armed with an appointment card, a determined expression and more bling than a gold-loving gangsta.

'Fancy a trip to Walthamstow? I've got a lead.'

'Shame you haven't got a dog as well then.' I looked him

up and down before demanding, 'Did you mug a Christmas cracker salesman on the way over here?'

His face was blank. 'What?'

Waving an arm, I gestured at the chains around his neck. 'What's with the metal-wear?'

He waggled the card. 'You'll understand in a minute.'

I squinted at it, trying to make out what it was for. 'Don't tell me. You're meeting a builder called Dave for drinks and want me to chaperone.'

He threw me a level look. 'I'm glad you're feeling better.'

I responded with a sunny smile. 'What's in Walthamstow?'

'Micky Snake, the best tattooist in London.'

'I bet that's not his real name.'

'Probably not,' Jeremy agreed. 'But he is the best. He doesn't let you into his studio unless he thinks you're serious about getting a tattoo.'

He sounded like a bundle of fun. 'How are we going to get in, then?'

Waggling the rectangle of card, Jeremy said, 'By pretending I'm a homie who wants a tattoo.' My mouth dropped into a horrified 'O', but Jeremy was oblivious. 'Come on, the appointment is at two o'clock.' He adopted what I guessed he thought was a brooding face. He looked like he was constipated. 'I don't think he'll be happy if we're late.'

Micky Snake's studio was about five minutes from the tube station, tucked away off the main road. Once we'd got past the complicated entry system and climbed the stairs to the first-floor studio, he showed us into his lair. We were the only customers there.

I gazed around in wonder. I'd never seen so many tattoos. Every bit of wall space was covered in drawings and photographs of body art. Micky himself was a walking advert for his job. His muscular arms and neck were thick with pictures, right up to his shaved head. He had none on his face. He'd gone for a thin moustache and goatee beard instead.

'I'm Micky,' he introduced himself, unnecessarily. 'Do you know what you're looking for, or did you want to have a look around the gallery?'

Jeremy took a seat on the black leather sofa and lifted one of the hefty ring-binders from the coffee table. 'I've got no idea. I'm hoping it'll leap out at us.'

Micky frowned. 'Us?'

'Me,' Jeremy amended quickly. 'I meant me.'

'I'll leave you to it.' Micky eyed Jeremy suspiciously. 'You'd better not be messing me about. I don't like time-wasters.'

With one final forbidding look, he stalked into another room and shut the door behind him. I pulled a face at his back. Tattoos weren't my thing, and anyone who had as many as Micky made me deeply uneasy. In fact, something about the whole set up was making me uncomfortable. I couldn't shake the feeling that something was trying to get my attention, but every time I tried to work out what it was, it skittered away.

A shiver crawled along my spine. 'I don't like it here.'

'Let's get on with it then. Have a look over my shoulder while I turn the pages. With a bit of luck we'll hit the jackpot, and when he comes back I'll tell him I can't find anything I like.'

My sense of unease increased with each page I saw, but I forced myself to keep looking, stomach tight with anxiety. As I stared down at the pages, an image started to flash in my mind's eye. I tried to blink it away, but it was persistent, and each time it stayed in my imagination for longer.

The scene was gloomy. A muffled figure stood in front of me. I couldn't make out his features. He raised an arm and a shiny blade flashed in the dim lights. It streaked towards me. As it did, the sleeve of his coat fell back, revealing a black tattoo. My eyes widened and I stumbled to my feet, backing away from Jeremy in horror.

'That one,' I whispered, pointing a shaking finger at an image on the page in front of us. 'The ace of spades.'

Jeremy didn't ask if I was sure. The look on my face must have said it all. His own expression tense, he dipped his head towards me once.

'Micky?' he called over one shoulder. 'Have you got a minute?'

The tattooist came through from the other room, rubbing his hands on an ink-stained cloth. 'You've decided, then?'

'Not exactly,' Jeremy said and pointed at the book. 'What can you tell me about this one?'

Micky glanced downwards at the image of the playing

card. 'A very popular choice. The ace is considered lucky, and the ace of spades is the luckiest card of them all. Some people combine it with the number thirteen.'

The room swam before my eyes. I jammed them shut, forcing down a tidal wave of fear. With sick realisation, I knew why the number on Jeremy's front door had bothered me so much. It had been my subconscious brain trying to warn me. As clearly as if it was painted on Micky's hairy forearm, I saw the tattoo on my killer's skin. It was the ace of spades, and snaked around the central spade was an inky thirteen.

Chapter 18

'On a scale of one to ten, how much does it hurt?'

Jeremy rubbed his right shoulder. 'I've had worse.'

Maybe he had, but I bet that didn't ease the pain. Micky Snake hadn't taken the news of Jeremy's change of heart very well. He'd called him 'rubber-necking tourist scum', following that with a string of swear words, some of which were new to me. I stored them away for future use. After he'd let rip with a few more curses, Micky had twisted Jeremy's arm up his back and marched him down the stairs to the street.

We made our way back to the Underground. 'At one point, I thought he was going to pin you down and brand you for life. Still, at least he didn't nick your bling.'

Jeremy threw me a dark look and said nothing. I

shrugged. Still shaken by the flashback to my death, I wasn't in the mood for chit-chat anyway.

By the time we reached the loo, the shops were closing and Jeremy was late for work.

'Are you sure you'll be all right?' he asked, catching my troubled glance down the shadowy steps. 'You can come to the theatre if you promise not to try any Lucifer-baiting.'

I shook my head. The last thing I needed was to get anyone suspicious again. 'Nah, go ahead. I'll be fine.'

He took some persuading, but eventually he went. I waited until I was sure he'd gone before I took myself off to Regent's Street. Window-shopping wasn't the most fun I could imagine having, but it beat hanging around on my own. Maybe by the time I'd finished lapping up the gadgets in the window of Hamleys, Ryan would have finished up at the Dearly D.

Eventually, I couldn't put off going home and turned my reluctant feet in that direction. Ryan had texted to say he was going to be busy for another hour or so. Hep hadn't replied to my message at all. Immediately after the Kimberly incident, she'd been great, spending a lot of her time making sure I was OK. Over the last few days, though, I'd noticed her slipping more and more into her own emotional world, and I got the impression it wasn't a particularly nice place to be. Whatever was going on in her head, she couldn't help the rage from spilling out into violent gestures, and she often sent traffic cones soaring with a well-aimed boot. How was she keeping a lid on things at home if she was this angry all the time?

I wasn't on my own long. Jeremy popped back after his shift had finished. The rush of happiness I got at seeing him appear in the doorway caught me by surprise. When had I become so attached to him?

'Have you noticed anyone hanging around here lately?' he said, after making me laugh with a description of that night's performance.

'Other than the usual assortment of weirdos and nutters, you mean?'

'I assume you're not lumping me in with that lot but, yes, other than them?'

I thought about it before shaking my head. 'Nope. Now that movie star has stopped stalking me I haven't seen anyone hanging around. Why?'

An unreadable expression flitted over his face. 'I got chatting to Gonzo, the homeless guy upstairs. He told me to be careful. Apparently, he's seen someone watching the comings and goings here.'

I stared at him. 'Who would be interested in a public toilet? You don't think Elvira's got ants in her pants again, do you?'

He shook his head. 'Gonzo says it was a man. He only really noticed him because the guy was standing in the doorway of the Tommy Hilfiger shop when he was ready to settle down for the night. Ripper didn't like the smell of him.'

Ripper was Gonzo's dog, a greyhound who'd been abandoned when he couldn't race any more. His deep brown eyes were intelligent and he certainly seemed to see me. Anyone he didn't like sounded suspicious in my book. Except for Jeremy, what kind of saddo loitered around public toilets, anyway?

'It might be the police doing surveillance,' I suggested doubtfully. 'I haven't noticed any drug deals going on, but they aren't to know that.'

Jeremy sniffed. 'It'd be easier if you had. They definitely weren't interested in my serial killer theory.' He paused in thought. 'It's probably nothing. Why don't you have a scout around later? If Gonzo's right, we need to know about it.'

'OK,' I said, thinking that I wasn't at all sure I needed to know anything of the sort. 'Before you go, I have a favour to ask.'

He raised an eyebrow.

'Actually, I have two favours to ask,' I amended. 'First, can you teach me how to do that eyebrow thing?'

A wry smile quirked Jeremy's lips. 'I'll try.'

'Second, if Hep agrees, would you be willing to talk to her parents?'

Understandably, he looked surprised at this last request. I'd never asked him to do anything like it before, mostly because I thought it would put him in an unbearable position. Imagine visiting a bereaved family and telling them you had a message from their dead loved one. I knew the psychics from the Dearly D did it sometimes, but Jeremy wasn't a hardened spiritualist. If Hep hadn't been worrying me so much I would never have put him on the spot.

'To say what?' Jeremy's voice was gentle. 'Do you think they're ready to hear what she wants to tell them?'

'They will if they value what's left of their ornament collection. I think Hep plans on breaking one a day for the next month.'

'Do you know why she's so angry?'

I sighed. There was a strong possibility I'd got it completely wrong, but I couldn't help feeling the reason Hep was still on earth was somehow connected to her parents. I knew she'd killed herself to find peace and wanted to pass across, but while she still blamed them for her death, she would always be angry and none of them could rest. As much as I'd miss her when she went, things couldn't go on as they were.

'I'm not sure. She told me once they never understood how bad the bullying was.'

Compassion flickered in his eyes. 'Check with Hep first. If it's what she wants, I'll do it.'

Several days went by before I got the chance to ask Hep about it. She wasn't answering texts, and no one had seen her at the Dearly D. Finally, I tracked her down in the park bandstand near her parents' house. It was a good thing I did. The local hoodie gang might have been permanently traumatised from the treatment she was about to dish out to them.

'You can't set fire to their cider bottle, Hep,' I told her firmly, dragging her away from temptation. 'No matter how much they swear.'

'I hate them.' She spat at their oblivious backs. 'They don't deserve to be alive.'

'Maybe not, but that isn't up to us.' I paused and took a nervous breath. 'I want to talk to you about something, and you might not like what I'm going to say. In fact, I can't think of much you'd like less.'

I explained. As I expected, she refused point blank to take part. It took me the best part of the afternoon to persuade her otherwise.

'It won't achieve anything,' she said, once her initial torrent of rage had subsided.

'You might feel better,' I offered, wondering if she'd read between the lines and realised what this might mean.

She aimed a half-hearted punch at a shrivelled balloon tied to one of the pillars. 'They didn't listen to me when I was alive,' she mumbled. 'It'll be even easier to ignore me now I'm dead.'

Somehow, I didn't think her parents were ignoring her, not with the amount of poltergeist activity she was generating around them, but I didn't say so. I was determined to get the three of them communicating, no matter how long it took.

Hep's mum and dad were older than I expected. Even allowing for the aging effect of their grief, I guessed they were in their fifties. They sat in their faded, flowery living room and stared at Jeremy, sorrow hanging around them like an accustomed blanket.

'How did you say you knew Rosemary?' Mrs Muldoon

asked, after Jeremy had introduced himself.

Nervously, he cleared his throat. 'I didn't, Mrs Muldoon.'

I gave him an encouraging nod. What he was doing was incredibly hard, and neither of us knew how it would go or even whether Hep was going to play ball. At the moment, she was sitting in the corner of the room, scowling ferociously and peeling the wallpaper from the wall.

'I'd like to start by saying I'm truly sorry for your loss.' Jeremy glanced from one to the other. 'I can only imagine what you've been through.'

Mrs Muldoon bowed her head. 'No one should outlive their child.'

Her husband said nothing.

'My purpose for coming here might seem hard to believe at first. If I was in your shoes I'm not sure I'd be able to accept it.' Jeremy paused and took a great gulp of what must now have been lukewarm tea. 'It might come as something of a shock to hear this, but your daughter is in this room right now.'

A ball of crumpled wallpaper sailed over our heads and bounced off the chimney breast. Mr and Mrs Muldoon didn't bat an eyelid. I guessed it was an everyday event for them.

If I'd been either of Hep's parents, the temptation to make a sarcastic comment at that moment would have been too great to resist. Neither of them said a word. Somehow, they didn't seem the sarcastic type. Instead, they continued to gaze at Jeremy as though he'd told them it was raining outside.

He went on. 'She's quite angry. My purpose today is to speak on Hep's – sorry, Rosemary's – behalf.'

Mrs Muldoon's expression softened. 'Can you see her?' she asked, wistful longing creeping into her voice.

Tears sprang into my eyes. The emotion on her face was heart-wrenching. No matter what Hep felt, in that moment I knew she had been loved by her mum and dad. They might not have told her so, but she'd been the centre of their world. The tragedy was, Hep had never known.

It was too complicated to explain how Jeremy knew about Hep. We'd agreed beforehand that it would be easier to pretend he could see her. With a questioning glance at me, he said gently, 'She's over by the fish tank.'

Silent tears spilled down Mrs Muldoon's worn cheeks. 'I'd give anything to be able to see her one last time.'

'Oh for pity's sake, it's like being on a daytime TV show,' Hep sneered from her corner. 'Any minute now they're going to wheel out the brother I never knew I had.'

It was an act. I could tell by her glistening eyes that she was struggling not to cry. 'Let go, Hep. You don't have to pretend any more.'

She stared hard at the patterned carpet, pressing her lips together. 'What do you know about it? You never wanted to die.'

I couldn't argue. It didn't mean I couldn't understand the depth of her desolation and loneliness, though. I knew how that felt. She'd thought killing herself would stop all the pain and bewilderment she felt at a world which seemed unable to accept her. Instead, things had got worse.

'No, but there are still things I wish I'd told my family. This is your chance, Hep. They're listening now.'

The words broke the last barrier. All the pent-up emotions she'd been forcing back in the months since her death came surging out. Jeremy paled, but did his best to translate the waves of utter misery I relayed to him.

'I couldn't escape the bullies!' she spat bitterly. 'They hounded me at school and followed me home, calling me names on the bus. They even sent me bitchy texts, always from different numbers so I couldn't grass. And . . . and then they posted a video of me having an asthma attack during cross-country on the internet.'

'Slow down, Hep,' I pleaded as she paused to suck in another impassioned breath. 'I can't keep up!'

She couldn't help herself, though. Mrs Muldoon openly sobbed. Her husband tried to comfort her, even though it was clear he, too, was feeling the force of the charged atmosphere. Zooming around over our heads were all the movable objects in the room. They sped up with every sentence, until they were little more than a blur. Jeremy and Hep's parents shrank lower into their seats.

'Why didn't they help?' Hep's voice was raw as she bellowed the words into the air, the lightbulbs flickering in their sockets. 'All I needed was their support.'

Mr Muldoon broke his silence for the first time to answer. 'We didn't know it was so bad,' he whispered raggedly. 'We'd have given our own lives to help, but how could we do anything if she didn't tell us? When the school admitted at the inquest what had been going on, I couldn't believe we hadn't noticed.' His anguished gaze dropped. 'Maybe it was easier not to see.'

'That's not true,' wept Mrs Muldoon. 'I was her mother, the one meant to keep her safe. All the signs were there. I just didn't understand what they meant.'

Hep reached boiling point. 'It's too late for this! Don't you get it? You can't make things right. No one can!'

She screamed a desperate cry of soul-wrenching unhappiness. The flying ornaments shattered, showering us with dust and broken china.

In the emptiness that followed, all I could hear was shallow breathing.

'I'm sorry we let you down, Rosie,' Mrs Muldoon said at last. 'Sometimes, I wake up thinking it's all been a horrible dream. Then I go into your room and you're not there.' Her voice caught and broke. 'Our lives ended the day you died. We miss you so very much.'

My gaze rested on Hep's down-turned head. Surely she wasn't immune to her parents' pain?

'How could I have messed up so badly, Lucy?' she whispered.

I crossed the room and knelt beside her, threading a comforting arm around her. There was no hatred in her now. 'You didn't, Hep.'

She watched her parents consoling each other for a

moment. When she spoke, her voice was dull. 'I've put them through hell.'

I considered my next words carefully. There was no denying that Hep had caused herself and her parents untold misery, but there must have been a way for their pain to end. An idea appeared in my head. Without thinking, I went with it.

'I've never told anyone this.' Sucking in a slow, deep breath, I carried on before my nerve broke. 'For a long time, I blamed my parents for what happened to me. Then I realised that I wasn't being fair. I chose to go to the party and I decided not to wait around for a cab. Eventually I saw that all my choices were my own.'

She stared down at her chipped black fingernails. 'It's easier to blame them.'

'Is it? I don't think so. Look at what it's doing to you.' I reached out and touched her cheek. 'Do you want to spend eternity blaming them?'

For several long seconds she didn't speak. I waited. Finally, she let out a puff of reluctant acknowledgement. 'All this time I kidded myself it was their fault. It wasn't, though, was it? How could it have been when I never gave them the chance to help?'

Tears dripped on to Mrs Muldoon's faded cardigan as she wrapped it around herself. 'Please forgive us, love. We never wanted you to leave.'

Millimetre by millimetre, Hep's head moved upwards as she came to terms with her new knowledge. Incredibly, the faintest of watery smiles crept over her face. 'It's OK, Mum,' she said, stretching out a hand towards her parents. 'I understand everything now. There's nothing to forgive.'

Mrs Muldoon's head jerked up. Her mouth dropped open. 'Rosie?'

Hep's eyes widened. 'You can hear me?'

A look of wonder spread over Mrs Muldoon's damp face. 'I can hear you, my darling. Can you, George?'

Finally, Mr Muldoon allowed his tears to escape. He pressed his lips together, nodding. 'I love you, Rosemary.'

I turned to Hep, wondering what was coming next. An uneasy frown settled on my forehead. 'Hep? You're glowing.'

It wasn't coming from her beaming smile. Bathed in a golden light, she had the tiniest of twinkling lights floating in her hair and all around her. With a jolt, I realised I could see through her.

'It's happening, Lucy. I'm passing across.' Her smile didn't falter as she gazed at me. 'It doesn't look half bad there.'

There was hardly anything left of her as she turned to her parents. 'I love you, Mum and Dad. Don't be sad any more. We'll see each other again.'

The words were little more than a whisper. A heartbeat later, the light faded away and she was gone.

For a long moment nobody spoke. Then Jeremy looked around at the fragments of broken china. 'With the benefit of hindsight, maybe we should have moved the breakable things out of here first.'

A wobbly smile crept over my face. 'Too late now, don't you think?'

Hep's dad chuckled sadly. 'Actually, she's done me a favour. I never liked the blasted things anyway.'

Jeremy and I didn't talk much on the way home. He seemed exhausted by his role in the evening's events, and I was in no mood for conversation. Apart from being stunned by Hep's sudden departure, the effect on her parents had made me think of my own mum and dad. They must have been grieving for me still. Did they need the emotional closure which catching my killer would bring? I couldn't know for sure, but I suspected they did. It was another reason to help Jeremy with his search. Pretty soon I was going to run out of ways to stall.

Chapter 19

As you might guess, Hep left a massive hole in my existence. A few months earlier we'd never met, and now I had to get used to the fact that when my phone vibrated it would never be with a text from her. Even though I knew she'd gone to a better place, it felt like she'd died all over again. Ryan suggested we have a party to celebrate her passing. It was a thoughtful idea, but in the end I said no. Hep had despised almost everyone. She wouldn't want them standing around pretending to be nice in her honour. We gatecrashed a gig at Wembley Arena instead. As we danced alongside sixty thousand emotionally challenged teens, I had the definite feeling Hep was smiling. Wherever she'd gone, she approved.

* * *

Events at Hep's house had driven all thoughts of my mysterious visitor out of my head. It wasn't until I saw someone lurking in the stairway a few days later that I remembered Gonzo's warning about the man he'd seen.

It was a little after midnight. I was on my way to the cupboard, thinking it was time I got some sleep, when I spotted him. He might have passed for someone looking to have a wee if it hadn't been for the furtive way he crouched on the bottom step to look around. It dawned on me he was trying to see if there were any security cameras. Instantly, I was suspicious and decided to see what he did next.

Obviously satisfied he wasn't being filmed, the man straightened up and crept down the last stair. I waited, wondering if he was checking the place out for a potential drug deal. One of the fluorescent lights had broken overhead, making the toilet gloomier than normal. I couldn't make out much detail, but he was dressed in what looked like black combat trousers and a dark jacket. He had a baseball cap pulled low over his face. As he stood silently in the centre of the room, I moved closer. There was definitely something odd about his behaviour. No one ever came in to soak up the atmosphere.

He had his back to me. I edged forwards, deciding at the very least I could get a description fixed in my mind, but every sense was screaming that something was wrong with this picture. If I could just put my finger on what it was . . .

Slowly, he turned round, and my brain caught up with what my body had been trying to tell it. I knew this man.

His face had haunted my dreams. Nine months ago he'd dragged me down to this toilet. For a nanosecond, I stared into the eyes of my killer.

My nerve broke. I bolted. Stumbling up the stairs, I gulped in rasping breaths of air. I ran past Gonzo, curled up in his shop doorway. Ripper saw me go and barked once. I didn't stop. Running faster than I'd ever managed at sports day, I fled to the first person who'd made me feel safe. It might have been wrong to enter his flat uninvited, but I was past caring. Cocooned in a corner of the sofa and surrounded by cushions, I closed my eyes and forced the nightmare away. That was how Jeremy found me when he got up for work the next morning.

'I think we should organise a stake-out,' Jeremy said when I explained what happened. 'If we're going to catch this guy, we need hard evidence to take to the police. That's why they refused to listen last time.'

I rolled my eyes. In the cold light of day, it didn't seem so bad. 'You've been watching the True Crime channel again.'

'Actually, it's not a bad idea,' Ryan chipped in. I hadn't wanted to drag him into things, but Jeremy had insisted.

'You would say that,' I muttered, feeling a bad mood beginning to take hold. I'd half hoped they'd tell me I was being ridiculous. By taking me seriously they were scaring me.

'Why has he waited so long to come back?' Jeremy wondered.

'How am I supposed to know?' I snapped. 'Maybe he's been drowning his bloodlust at flower-arranging classes.'

'Or maybe he's been in prison for something else,' Jeremy said in a more reasonable tone.

Ryan's expression was grim. 'Then he'll be right at home when we send him back there.'

I didn't like the idea of a stakeout, but Jeremy and Ryan couldn't wait to start playing cops and robbers. With my reluctant involvement, they split the evenings into guard shifts. Gonzo was easily bribed to keep watch at ground level. We were ready. All we had to do was wait.

Another week passed by. By the time the toilets closed at three o'clock each morning, I knew the killer wasn't coming and packed Jeremy off home before he got locked in. Ryan stayed with me every night. I wasn't complaining. Since our trip to the zoo I couldn't get enough of kissing him, and although I could have wished for more romantic surroundings, once my initial anxiety had dropped, I enjoyed spending the night in his arms. I hated it when he had to leave me, though.

The next night was following the same pattern as all the others. It was one-fifteen a.m. Jeremy was struggling to keep his eyes open as he perched on the toilet in the end cubicle, leaning against the wall. For a supposed night-owl, he certainly liked a good kip. Gonzo had reported nothing unusual and Ripper was quiet. It looked as though it was going to be another no-show. I was relieved.

'Why don't you call it a night, Sleeping Beauty?'

He woke up, fixing me with a bleary gaze. 'Eh?'

'Go home.'

He nodded and started to get to his feet.

'Shhh!' Ryan's muttered warning carried clearly over the tiles. 'Someone's coming!'

I held up a hand to Jeremy. 'Wait. Can you hear anything?'

He tilted his head to one side and listened. His eyes flew to mine instantly. Ryan was right – someone was making their way down the stairs. I held my breath.

The footsteps stopped. Taking a deep breath, I leaned out of the cubicle to look. And froze. It was him.

Jeremy inched forwards, peering through the crack in the cubicle door.

'What are you doing?' I muttered anxiously. 'He'll see you.'

It was already too late. Catching the flicker of movement in the corner of his eye, the man spun round and strode purposefully to where we were hidden. He pushed the door and gazed coldly inside, hands in pockets.

'You shouldn't be down here.' The man's voice was raspy and laced with menace. 'This is my special place.'

The last sentence caused a violent shiver to run down my spine. He'd said the same words to me on New Year's Eve, a chilling smile on his lips as he'd eaten up the shadowy space between us. It was the exact moment I'd known something was wrong, and it made me suddenly fearful for Jeremy.

Thrusting out his chin and looking both terrified and

furious, Jeremy said, 'I know what you did. I've told the police about you.'

A terrified groan escaped me. What was he thinking? He was no match for a killer. I couldn't imagine what made the man want to maim and murder, but I did know that Jeremy was in grave danger and there was nothing I could do to help. Or was there?

Darting forwards, I grabbed Ryan's hand. 'Help me!'

Concentrating, I smacked the palm of my hand hard on to the tap in the first sink. Water gushed out. I moved on to the next one. Ryan caught on quickly and did the same at the other sinks. Soon all the taps were roaring and the man was staring at them in confusion.

'Run, Jeremy!'

He didn't. Instead of using the diversion to get away from the lunatic, I watched in horrified disbelief as Jeremy picked up the newly broken toilet seat from the floor of cubicle one and raised it high over his head. He'd obviously lost it. Did he seriously think a piece of cracked plastic was going to help? My killer saw the action reflected in the mirror and turned, drawing his hand from his pocket at the same time.

'Look out!' I screamed.

The momentum of his swing carried Jeremy forward. Almost in slow motion, the man drew his arm back. His sleeve dropped to his elbow. The outline of the ace of spades tattoo was dark against his pale skin. A glint of silver flashed in the flickering light and Jeremy's eyes widened in sudden shock. Barely visible against his jacket, a knife was sunk deep into his chest.

He took a few staggering steps backwards before dropping heavily to his knees. Twitching helplessly, his fingertips brushed at the knife handle, trying to tug it from the wound. With an effort, his fingers gripped it. I ran to him. White-faced, Ryan followed. The knife clattered from Jeremy's numb hand and skidded into the shadows beneath the basins. He toppled backwards, unconscious.

Ice-cool and emotionless, his attacker stared down for several long seconds. Then, without another glance, he stepped over Jeremy's shuddering body and walked up the stairs.

Chapter 20

Time stood still. Caught in my own nightmarish memories, it felt like an age before I found my voice and started barking instructions at Ryan.

'Go for help,' I commanded, summoning all my strength to drag Jeremy's limp hand on to the wound to try and stop the bleeding. 'Hurry!'

'I don't want to leave you.'

I looked up fiercely. 'We can't help him on our own. The best we can do is raise the alarm. Do you know where any of the Dearly D psychics live?'

He nodded. 'Will you be OK?'

My expression was grim. 'I will be. I'm not so sure about him.'

Moments later, Ryan was gone. I did my best to assess

the wound. It was hard to see much in the half-light but I couldn't help wishing Jeremy had left the knife in his chest. It might have stemmed the shocking amount of sticky redness pooling on the floor beside me. The shallowness of his breathing scared me too. I stared down at his pale face. For the first time since my death, I prayed someone would come to use the toilet. It didn't matter who, as long as it wasn't Jeremy's attacker, returning to finish the job.

Minutes ticked by. It seemed like Ryan had been gone ages. I hadn't thought to ask how far he had to go and had no idea how long help would be. I couldn't even remember if Gonzo and Ripper were sleeping upstairs. Maybe I should try and get a message to the dog, but I didn't want to leave Jeremy. In the meantime, I watched the dark red stain on Jeremy's jacket grow and seep on to the tiled floor. My arm ached from the pressure of holding Jeremy's hand over the cut. I couldn't keep it up much longer. If help didn't arrive soon I would have to think of something else to stem the bleeding.

Jeremy's eyelids fluttered. How could I keep him with me? Without a clue what to say, I started talking, producing meaningless sentences simply to make noise. I hadn't come out with so much waffle since my Year Nine French oral exam.

'I'm sorry I got you into this,' I murmured, gazing down at his grey face. 'You've done so much for me. Please don't die.'

His hand fell away as I let it go, unable to hold on any longer. Instantly, blood welled up. I bit my lip. How much longer would Ryan be? Could Jeremy last that long?

I scrambled to my feet, reaching a decision. It was time to try and persuade Ripper to wake Gonzo up.

'Hold on, Jeremy. I'll be back.'

The dog was already alert. His head rose as I stumbled up the last step and he let out a tiny, questioning whine.

'Ripper! Wake Gonzo up!'

He tilted his head to one side, letting out a single bark.

'Come on, boy, we don't have long. Make some noise!'

Seeming to understand, he let out a volley of barks. Gonzo opened his eyes and sat up. 'What's up, Ripper?'

'Good dog!' I cried. All I had to do now was persuade him to drag Gonzo downstairs and we were in business.

It wasn't as easy as it sounds. Realising the dog was in a frenzy about something, Gonzo couldn't make out what it was and cast around for clues. Ripper didn't want me to get too close and backed away with an anxious, whining snarl. Almost crying with frustration, I gave up. There had to be another way. In a city where millions lived and worked, there must be someone who could help. All I needed was for one of them to hear me.

My panic-stricken footsteps took me to Oxford Street. Even in the early hours of the morning, it was busy. I ran from person to person, begging them to help. Each time, they looked straight through me. Tears streamed down my face. Jeremy was going to die if I didn't do something. In desperation, I raised my head skywards and let out a scream of pure anguish.

'What's the matter? Why are you screaming?'

I closed my mouth abruptly and spun round to find the speaker. It was a woman, around Jeremy's age, and she was staring right at me, her face twisted in concern.

'I'm a ghost. Can you see me?'

It seemed like a ridiculous question, but after the Elvira incident I wasn't taking any chances.

'I'm a psychic and I can see you're a very unhappy ghost. What's wrong?'

I almost fainted in relief. 'Dial 999. There's a man in the toilets on Carnaby Street. He's been stabbed.'

Her colour drained away. Fumbling in her bag, she hauled out a phone and did as I asked.

'Show me,' she demanded as soon as the call was finished.

Thanking my lucky stars, I turned and led the way, praying it wasn't too late.

Apart from my own, I'm not massively familiar with stabbings. I did know that one cut in the wrong place was enough to kill. Was Jeremy's wound fatal? He'd lost a lot of blood. His face was ashen by the time we got back to the toilet. He hadn't moved.

My angel of mercy went straight into action. Calmly, she swept her hair back out of the way and knelt at Jeremy's side. Without a second thought, she shrugged off her expensive-looking cardigan and crumpled it into a ball. She eased it over the wound and pressed down firmly. Her other hand travelled to his neck.

'His pulse is weak but steady,' she said after a minute. 'It's a good job you found him when you did.'

I couldn't find the words to explain. Thankfully, I didn't have to. A pair of heavily booted feet thudded down the stairs, closely followed by another. The paramedics didn't waste any time.

'Stand back please, miss.'

One of them checked Jeremy over with professional coolness, cutting away the layers of clothing to reveal an ugly puncture on the right side of his chest. The other shook out the stretcher he carried and laid it out on the floor. I watched, gripped by an overwhelming tension.

'It looks like he's going to be OK.' The paramedic kneeling next to Jeremy looked up at the young woman. 'Any idea what happened?'

I hadn't thought that far ahead. It made sense for the woman to say no. The police would be arriving at any minute. If she said yes, she'd be sucked into an investigation and any chance at slipping quietly away would be lost. Her gaze slid towards me.

I summoned a grateful smile. 'You've done enough. I'll understand if you want to go.'

It might have been my imagination, but she seemed to shake her head the tiniest bit. Her eyes stayed fixed on mine. She wasn't going anywhere.

'OK. His name is Jeremy Parker. Tell them he came down to use the loo and didn't come out. You came down to check on him and found him like this.'

As she repeated the words to the paramedic, I let out a sigh of relief. Now that I knew Jeremy was out of immediate danger there were a whole load of other things crowding into my mind for attention. Having another psychic around was going to be so helpful.

'I assume you'll want to come to the hospital,' said the paramedic. 'The police will need to talk to you, but they can catch up with you there.'

She nodded. 'I'm Celestine,' she added helpfully, for my benefit.

The paramedic threw her a polite look. 'Good for you, love. Move back a bit and we'll get him on to the stretcher.'

During our ride in the ambulance, I gave Celestine the bones of what had happened. Not everything, but enough information to satisfy her obvious curiosity and enough so that she could pass on a description of my killer to the police. I couldn't be totally sure she wasn't going to sell me down the river like Elvira had, but she'd earned the right to know how Jeremy got hurt, especially if she was going to have to lie to the police about it. Although she absorbed the news in silence, I could tell she had questions. Later, I might have to answer them.

With a sudden gasp, I remembered Ryan. Whipping my phone out, my fingers flew over the buttons. He'd be out of his mind with worry and I wanted him to meet me at the hospital. After the events of the evening, I was in serious need of a hug.

Once the message was safely winging its way towards him, I looked up. Celestine was frowning quizzically at me.

'I'm texting my boyfriend. He went for help, I want to tell him to come to the hospital.'

Her eyebrows shot up.

I grinned. 'Oh yeah, we've got ghostly mobiles. Some of us even manage to have love lives. There's probably a lot you don't know about the afterlife.'

She winked. The odds against finding another psychic when I needed one had to be enormous. Maybe it was fate, although I doubted there was a god of lighting engineers. However I'd managed it, I had a good feeling about her. I glanced over at Jeremy, pale and unconscious underneath his red blanket. My relief evaporated. He'd been stabbed and it was because of me. Now I was involving someone else. She'd saved Jeremy's life, but I shouldn't be confiding in Celestine. I couldn't afford to involve any more innocent people.

Chapter 21

I've never liked hospitals. The ones I'd been in were either too hot or too cold and smelled awful. Throw in the risk of contracting some disgusting flesh-eating bug and you've got the last place you'd want to go if you were ill. Obviously the chances of my picking up any deadly germs were infinitesimally small, but it didn't make the place any less grim.

University College Hospital wasn't the worst one I'd been to. The atmosphere in the intensive care unit was hushed, punctuated by low voices and mysterious beeps from the equipment. Not long after we'd arrived, a doctor had appeared, briefly, to advise Celestine that Jeremy's condition was stable. We didn't know more than that. Celestine and I sat in the deserted waiting area, neither saying much. Occasionally another ghost passed through, but none of them paid us much attention. Celestine flicked through an out-of-date magazine someone had left on the worn fabric seat, one that I'd read already. Jeremy had brought it to me the previous month.

I studied Celestine as she turned the dog-eared pages. She was very pretty. I'd guessed at first she was the same age as Jeremy, but now I had time to look at her properly, I thought she was a few years younger. With her blond hair tucked behind her ears, she didn't seem that much older than me.

'I'm twenty-five.'

My mouth dropped. 'Exactly how psychic are you?'

'I've been able to see ghosts since I was little. I don't read minds, but in this case I don't have to. You're trying to work me out.'

It wasn't the first time I'd wondered why Jeremy could only see me, but I had a more important question. 'Actually, I was wondering if you've got a boyfriend.'

Celestine laughed. 'Not at the moment.'

A half-smile crossed my face as my idea took shape. If everything worked out the way I planned, she wouldn't be single for long.

By the time Ryan arrived at three a.m., Jeremy was out of intensive care and in a side room off the main ward. There wasn't time for more than a hurried introduction between him and Celestine. The police were hovering, eager to find out the details of what had happened, but Jeremy was sleeping and the nurses refused to let them near him. They turned their attention to Celestine. With our help, she sailed through the questions, keeping the details as vague as possible, apart from her description of my killer. It made sense to pretend she'd been on a first date with Jeremy and didn't know him very well.

'I think that's all we need for now,' the dark-suited detective said, closing his notebook. 'You'll be here for a while, if there's anything else?'

Celestine hesitated for a fraction of a second, and I wondered if she regretted getting involved. Then she nodded. 'I'll be here.'

'Lucy?' Jeremy's voice sounded painfully weak as his eyelids fluttered open.

'Hey,' I said, abandoning my game of Paper, Scissors, Stone with Ryan and moving nearer to the bed. 'Good of you to join us.'

He gave a faint smile. 'Sorry. I told you, I'm too old for these late nights.'

I shook my head sorrowfully. 'I hate to tell you this, but the extra beauty sleep hasn't helped. You're still ugly.'

'Cut him some slack, Lucy. He's had a rough night,' Celestine joined in, her tone playful. 'Aren't you going to introduce us?'

Jeremy's eyes widened as he worked out the implications of the sentence. 'You – she – you found someone else who can see you!'

At least his brain still worked. 'Celestine, meet Jeremy.

166

Jeremy, this is Celestine. She kind of saved your life.'

Jeremy was silent for a moment as he stared at Celestine. 'Thank you,' he said finally.

Without dropping his gaze, Celestine replied, 'My pleasure. It's Lucy you should thank, though. She was the one who told me where you were.'

'And you came to the hospital?'

Celestine shrugged. 'Lucy needed someone to explain. There were no other psychics around so I got the job.'

Soon, they were chatting like they'd known each other forever. I glanced over at Ryan and nudged my head towards the door. Would they notice if we left them to it? Probably not. If I was honest, now that I knew Jeremy was going to be OK, I couldn't wait to get away. The hospital was giving me the heebie-jeebies. Besides, I wanted to get back to the toilet to see how the investigation was going.

Outside, Ryan touched my shoulder. 'Can we take a detour? There's someone I need to see.'

Mystified, I nodded and followed him along the corridor. Was there anywhere he didn't have friends?

A few minutes later, the awful truth dawned. The area of the hospital he led me to was a world away from the bustle of intensive care. The stillness was uncomfortable and the nurses padded around with sad efficiency. It wasn't a ghost Ryan wanted to visit. It was his dad.

'You can wait here if you like.' Ryan was pale but determined as he paused outside the door to a side room. 'His wounds have healed, but it's still not a pretty sight.'

The sadness in his eyes cut me. I wound my fingers around his and squeezed. 'I want to come in.'

You could have heard a pin drop inside the room. Every few seconds the air was split by the twin beeps of the life support machine and heart monitor. In the centre of the wires and regulation hospital bedding was the still figure of a grey-haired man. I stared in mute horror at the rise and fall of the respirator and the tiny blips of light on the screen. They were the only signs of life. My eyes grew damp. The machines might have kept him breathing, but he wasn't truly alive. Now I understood Ryan's need to help others. Whether he knew it or not, he was trying to make up for being unable to help his father. Maybe that was why he hadn't passed across.

'Has he ever woken up?' My whisper sounded harsh in the hushed atmosphere.

Ryan shook his head, his gaze glued to his dad's face. 'The worst thing is not knowing. He hasn't passed across, he isn't here, so where is he?' His hands jerked helplessly. 'In limbo? Trapped inside his own head? Wherever he is, I can't reach him.'

I laid soft fingers on his arm. 'Don't do this to yourself. It's not your fault.'

His eyes glittered. 'Yeah, I know. But I have to believe that one day I'll find him and bring him back. My mum needs that.'

I didn't trust myself to speak. What could I say, anyway? The depth of his pain was almost unbearable, and I wasn't surprised he kept it locked away. My heart ached for him, but I was also honoured that he'd shared his anguish. I gave him a fierce hug. 'Is there anything I can do to help?'

The faintest of smiles flickered around his lips as he turned to leave. 'You're already doing it. Come on, we'd better get back.'

Carnaby Street was closed to everyone except the police. Even Gonzo was gone, although his blanket was still there. I had a momentary pang at the thought of him sleeping somewhere without it and sent Ryan off on a walk around to see if he'd settled somewhere else for what was left of the night.

The toilet itself was almost deserted. Most of the crime team had been and gone. They'd found the knife and taken it away for testing. One last technician was dusting the taps for fingerprints, on the instruction of the shabby-coated detective who seemed to be in charge.

'Make sure you do all of them. Check for DNA evidence. Our boy might have washed the victim's blood off before he left.'

I thought back. He hadn't, but it wasn't the worst suggestion I'd heard. During the investigation into my murder I'd got to know most of the local police. I recognised the detective's face, although I didn't remember his name. The young police constable he was with looked no older than me and wore his uniform proudly. He had 'new recruit' written all over him.

'Wasn't there another stabbing here last year?' he asked.

The detective nodded. 'Yeah, a young girl. She died of multiple wounds. Nasty.'

'Do you think there might be a link?' The young officer looked thoughtful. 'Two knife incidents in the same place in such a short space of time? It could be someone who uses these toilets a lot.'

'No, they're completely different crimes. I reckon Mr Parker walked in on a drugs deal. The dealer attacked him to get away.'

'Still,' the policeman insisted. 'It might be worth some surveillance.'

'He'd be stupid to come back,' the detective said. 'If he's got any sense, he'll know we've found the knife. We've got other places that need surveillance more.'

Their voices died away as they moved up the stairs. Relief whooshed through me. Murderers were part of their everyday life – they knew more about them than me. If they said he wouldn't come back, then he probably wouldn't. Even though we'd lost this chance to catch him, I didn't care. If I was really being optimistic, maybe we'd even scared him enough to stop his brutal spree. I didn't even care if not catching him meant I couldn't pass across, as long as I never had to stare into those soulless eyes again. I didn't even mind spending eternity in a toilet, as long as I still had Ryan. It might not be Buckingham Palace, but at least now it felt safer.

Chapter 22

No one likes getting it wrong. I'm no different from anyone when it comes to the sinking realisation that something isn't how you thought it was. But it wasn't often I got things as badly wrong as I did after Jeremy's stabbing.

It was six o'clock on Sunday, a little over a week since the attack, and the police tape and serious crime signs were long gone. I'd managed to convince Ryan that it was fine for him to leave me and head over to the Dearly D. So when I heard the heavy tread of footsteps on the stairs and the tattooed man came into view, I was as alone as I had ever been. Somehow, seeing him in the daytime was even creepier. I shivered with shock and futile anger. I didn't know what he intended to do, but there wasn't a thing I could do to stop him.

I watched through narrowed eyes as he warily checked over his shoulder. Why had he come back? Surely he must have known that the police had found the knife. Then he closed his eyes and his mouth curved into a tender smile. With a burst of sick understanding, I realised what he was doing. By coming back to the toilets, he was reliving his hideous crimes.

'The blood was so beautiful,' he crooned, his voice so low I struggled to catch the words. 'Like glorious, scarlet roses blooming against the snow.' His eyes snapped open and his face hardened with sadistic pleasure.

A burst of bitter venom rose inside me. He made murder sound so trivial, something pretty to satisfy his savage urges, and I knew he intended to kill again. Something twisted in my heart, fed by hate. This man had stolen my future and broken the hearts of my family. When I thought about how many other lives he'd casually torn apart for his own twisted desires, my hatred burned more strongly. It had to end. No one else could die by his hand.

I knew exactly what to do. With ice-cold deliberation, I went to the first sink and pushed the tap down hard. Water gushed into the sink. The man froze. Slowly, he raised his head to stare at the sink. My steel gaze never leaving him, I moved on to the next tap and repeated the action. The second sink began to fill with water. By the time all six taps were flowing, he was standing still, a wary expression on his unshaven face.

'Have I got your attention yet?' I moved to stand in front

of him. With intense concentration, I tapped the brim of his baseball cap, sending it somersaulting upwards. 'Believe me, it's going to get worse. I'm just getting warmed up.'

He gasped and scrambled backwards to snatch the hat from the floor. 'Who's there?' he stammered.

Eyes darting left and right, he turned to leave. I was waiting at the bottom of the stairs. I should have known he was a coward. Apart from Jeremy, his victims had been young and trusting. He hadn't taken the chance that they would be able to fight back.

'You're nothing,' I snarled as another burst of cold fury shot through me and my palms smacked hard into his chest. Hep had been right when she said anger helped. I was about to make this man wish he'd never been born.

Whimpering, he picked himself up off the tiles and tried the stairs again. I lashed out a solid foot and he tripped, crunching painfully on to the first step. Rage gave me superstrength. With a furious howl, I seized his out-stretched trainer and heaved backwards. He flew across the room, crumpling against the urinal on the far side.

'Help! Somebody, help me!' he screamed, his voice thick.

'No one's coming to help you,' I thundered, pushing my face close to where he lay in a stunned heap. 'It's my turn now!'

I whirled around and slammed my fist into each of the cubicle doors. They crashed against their frames, echoing in the emptiness. Utterly enraged, I ripped the toilet-roll holders from the walls and sent tissue cascading across the ceiling. In the last cubicle I hauled the final metal toilet-roll holder from the wall and hurled it at the man's head with a shriek. It connected with a sickening thud.

Babbling in dazed incoherence, the man shook his head and fixed his eyes on the stairs. Fuelled by fear, he leapt to his feet and made a dash for the exit.

He reached the top of the stairs ahead of me and started off down the street. I paused, mind racing. Could I outrun him? Probably not, even in his injured state: he had terror to drive him. But if I didn't do something fast he'd get away, and this time, I knew he wouldn't be back. I spun in a wild circle, searching for any source of help. My eyes stopped in the doorway of a shop. Gonzo was there, staring after the man. Ripper was snarling, straining at the rope. In a flash, I knew what to do.

Dashing over to Gonzo, I concentrated once more and snatched the rope from his fingers.

'Go, Ripper! Get him!'

The greyhound didn't need to be told twice. Intent on his prey, he sped along the street. Gonzo let out a shout and raced after the dog. For the second time that week, I found myself running faster than I'd ever done before. Ripper was way ahead of us. He lunged forwards, teeth gnashing. Man and dog tumbled together. My killer lashed out with his foot, catching Ripper on the side of his head. The dog whimpered and let go.

'Oi!' Gonzo bellowed as he reached them. 'No one kicks my dog!'

He dived forwards, fists raining down on the man. Passers-by were stopping. I saw one punching numbers into a mobile phone. *Please be calling the police*, I prayed.

Obviously realising he was about to be caught, the man started desperately pummelling back and Gonzo was coming off worst. With so many witnesses there was no way I could do anything to help. Then I saw Celestine pushing her way to the front of the crowd. Sagging with relief, I caught her eye.

'It's him!' I bellowed. 'That's the man who attacked Jeremy!'

She understood. 'Someone call the police! That man tried to kill my boyfriend.'

Several people pulled out their phones and a few of the men dived forwards. They pulled Gonzo and my killer apart, gripping both of them tightly as they struggled.

'Not that one,' Celestine gestured at Gonzo. 'He's done nothing wrong.'

A loud wail split the air as a police van screeched to a halt. Officers piled out and rushed towards us. Some took hold of my murderer, others began asking what had happened.

Celestine stepped forward. 'My boyfriend was stabbed in those toilets seven nights ago. I saw that man running away.'

'Are you sure, miss?'

Celestine glanced at me. I nodded.

'Yes, it was definitely him. I'd know those tattoos any-where.' She lowered her voice, her eyes fixed on mine and filled with sadness. 'And that's not all. A young woman was stabbed to death in the same place last New Year's Eve. Unless I'm very much mistaken, this man was responsible. You're looking at the man who killed Lucy Shaw.'

Chapter 23

'How did you know?'

Even as I asked the question, I knew what Celestine's answer would be. Jeremy had told her. That was why she was on Carnaby Street. He'd sent her to make sure I was all right.

Celestine shifted on the edge of Jeremy's bed and gave a sad smile. 'I'm sure you don't need to ask. I wanted to know what was going on the night Jeremy got hurt. He explained, and in doing so, told me your story.'

'I'm glad you turned up when you did,' Ryan said, leaning back against the window. 'Lucy's killer might be walking around still if you hadn't.'

Jeremy looked thoughtful. 'We should tell Sarah her attacker has been caught. It'll do her good to know he's behind bars, and she might be able to identify him.'

I was feeling strangely empty. The see-saw emotions of the last few days were catching up with me. It wouldn't have taken much to burst my fragile self-control and set my tears free. Once I started, I wasn't sure I could stop.

'How are you feeling, Lucy?' Celestine turned concerned eyes on me. I didn't care what she said about her mind-reading skills, she guessed far too many of my thoughts for my liking.

I tried to summon a convincing smile. 'I'm OK.'

'Good.' Jeremy winced as he sat up. 'I'd hate to think I went through this for nothing.'

My sight shimmered with tears. 'You didn't.'

Ryan came over and put a protective arm around my shoulder. 'Hey, what's with the sadness? Everything worked out fine.'

I couldn't hold it back any longer. A heartfelt sob escaped me. 'I know and I'm ha-happy, really I am. It's a bit m-much to take in, that's all.'

They fussed around, trying to soothe me. I let them. It was either that or explain the real reason for my tears: I might have been relieved it was all over, but I was also petrified about what came next. We'd caught my killer, and although that brought me some peace, it also reminded me that Ryan was still tied to this world. If catching my killer meant leaving Ryan, then a tiny selfish part of me couldn't help wishing he'd got away.

Ryan glanced at the clock on the wall. 'It's visiting time.'

A spark of understanding passed between us. 'Do you

want to go and see her?' I asked Ryan.

Jeremy looked confused. 'What? See who?'

'Ryan's mum,' I supplied. 'She never misses an opportunity to visit his dad.'

Sympathy etched itself on Celestine's face. 'Off you go then. We'll be here when you get back.'

The room was dimly lit when we entered. A woman I guessed to be Ryan's mum was sitting beside the bed, reading from a sheet of paper.

'The lads at work said hi,' she said, her voice determinedly cheerful. 'Big Pete still says no one makes a cuppa quite like yours.'

I risked a glance at Ryan. His eyes were fixed on his mother. I could almost feel his pain. 'Have you tried talking to her?'

He sighed. 'She can't hear me. Neither of them can.'

I reached for his hand. 'At least you've tried.'

We listened in silence as Ryan's mother spilled out the details of her day. I knew she wasn't that old, but her greying hair and lined face made her look it. I supposed that was what the death of a loved one did – drained the life from the family they left behind – and already I knew what it did to the dead. Ryan's anguish was unbearable. I had to try and help.

'Sing to him.'

He stared at me. 'What?'

I gripped his fingers. 'Sing him a song. I read somewhere

music reaches coma victims more than talking.'

Unconvinced, he shook his head. 'I don't have a guitar.'

'You don't need one. What was his favourite song?'

His gaze straying back to his father's face, Ryan thought about it. 'Something by The Beatles, I guess. "Yesterday", maybe?'

'Try it,' I commanded, my voice soft. 'He taught you how to play so it must have mattered to him. What have you got to lose?'

After a few minutes, Ryan's mother seemed to run out of things to say.

'Here's your chance,' I whispered.

He hesitated. 'I don't know if I can.'

Pouring all the encouragement I could into my voice, I said, 'You can. He's waiting for you.'

The room was still for a moment longer. Then Ryan cleared his throat. Uncertainly, he began to sing.

He grew more confident as the verse went on, colouring each line with his pent-up sorrow and longing. By the time he reached the chorus, tears were running down my face and the strain of holding it together for so long, and for so many people, was showing in Ryan's glistening eyes. I gazed at the still figure on the bed, praying for a miracle. *Please hear him,* I begged silently, willing the unmoving eyelids to open. *Please come back.*

Listening to Ryan reach out to his dad was one of the most haunting and beautiful things I'd ever witnessed. He opened himself up more with every word and I knew he was holding nothing back, even though the strength of his emotions hurt. I had no idea if I was the only one who could hear the song or whether the music was working its magic. I hoped with all my heart it was.

As Ryan reached the end of the song. I scarcely dared to breathe. Ryan's head drooped exhausted on to his chest but his eyes were fixed on his father. For a moment, nothing happened. Then Ryan's mother let out a gasp. 'John?'

Her chair flew backwards and she stumbled to the doorway. 'Sister Margaret, come quickly! He squeezed my hand! I felt it!'

Ryan stepped forward, his expression intent. 'Dad?'

As we watched, one eyelid fluttered. Nurses crowded into the room. A second later, the other eye opened.

One of the nurses looked at Ryan's mum. 'It's a start. Why don't you say hello to your husband?'

She burst into tears. 'Oh, John.'

Whooping with delight, I threw my arms around Ryan. 'You did it!'

He tore his gaze away from his dad and smiled back. 'No, *we* did it. I'd never have thought of that on my own.'

'But it was you he came back to.'

Ryan glanced over at the crowded bed. 'Yeah. Maybe now they can put their lives back together.'

Thinking fleetingly of my own parents, I rested my head on his shoulder. 'I hope so.'

He took a final agonised look at his parents and swallowed. 'I think it's time we let them get started.'

* * *

Jeremy and Celestine were full of compassion.

'That was a lovely thing you did, Ryan,' Celestine said. 'And I'd be happy to speak to them someday, if you think it might help?'

'I'd like that, thank you.'

Jeremy looked at me, his pale face puzzled. 'I don't understand why you haven't passed over. We caught your killer.'

I didn't know what he expected me to say. It wasn't like I was working from a manual. Miserably, I stared at the floor.

'I had a thought about that. Do you believe in fate, Lucy?' Celestine was gazing at me, her blue eyes soft and warm.

I nodded, not trusting myself to speak.

'Me too.' She smiled and cast a veiled glance at Jeremy. 'I think you were here for a very specific reason, and it might not be just the one we all thought.'

Jeremy turned to meet her gaze and something extraordinary happened. I swear I saw a spark pass between them as a connection was made. Sharply, I looked from one to the other and understanding dawned. If Celestine was right, my real task hadn't been to stop a murderer. It had been to lead Jeremy to his soulmate.

'Did you see that?' I demanded of Ryan.

'Like magic, isn't it?' Head tilted to one side, he was watching me closely. 'Are you ready?'

He didn't need to explain what he meant.

'No,' I whispered, as the fear of losing him tightened its stranglehold. 'I don't want to go.'

'Don't fight it,' he said. 'I think it's time.'

Even though I knew he was right, my sorrow caused a lump to grow in my throat. I swallowed hard and nodded.

'You worried me, you know,' I told Jeremy. 'You're a total nightmare. How could I expect you to cope on your own?'

His gaze was suspiciously damp as he looked back at me. 'Don't worry, I'm going to be fine.' He reached out a hand to grasp Celestine's. 'We're both going to be just fine.'

'You have to promise to name your first child Lucy,' I said, tears streaming down my cheeks. 'Even if it's a boy.'

Celestine was crying too. 'We promise.'

I caught sight of my hands. They sparkled with a thousand twinkling lights. 'It's happening,' I sobbed. Blindly, I turned to Ryan. 'I can't leave you.'

He stood up and walked towards me. 'You don't have to,' he said, smiling softly. 'Look.'

I stared at his outstretched fingers and let out a ragged gasp. They were filled with the same glow as mine. 'You mean —?'

He grinned. 'Yep. There's no getting rid of me. Wherever we're heading, we're going there together.'

My sadness vanished in a searing burst of happiness. I turned my face upwards. 'You know,' I said in a low voice only he could hear, 'I've always wondered what it would be like to snog in another dimension.'

Ryan smiled down at me. 'That's quite a coincidence, actually. So have I.'

His lips lowered until they gently brushed against mine. A blaze of golden light blossomed all around us, and the final truth crystallised. It didn't matter where we were going next. I had Ryan, and in that one perfect moment, he was everything I needed.

Acknowledgements

In order to acknowledge everyone who had some input into this book, I'd have to thank pretty much everyone I've ever met because they all contributed something to how I view the world. However, narrowing it down slightly, the following people deserve a mention:

A teacher called Eugene Tumelty, now the headteacher of St Bernard's RC Secondary School, who encouraged a gawky teenager to believe that just maybe she had something special. Thanks, sir.

My dad, Phil, for setting the bar so high I needed a pogo stick to get over it and my mum, Meg, for teaching the eight-year-old me that if a job is worth doing, it's worth doing properly.

Pat Posner, who suffered my first draft and offered the best advice and support a fledgling writer could get. You are a star.

Jo Williamson at Antony Harwood Ltd, who is everything I could wish for in an agent. Thank you for taking a chance on Lucy and me, and for putting up with the literary equivalent of 'Are we nearly there yet?'.

Brenda, Ruth and Melissa at Piccadilly Press, who saw the glitter of gold under the dust and polished away until it gleamed. Thanks for making *My So-Called Afterlife* a reality.

My So-called Haunting

Tamsyn Murray

What's worse than being the new kid in school?
Being the new kid with a secret to hide . . .
like the ability to see ghosts.

When fourteen-year-old Skye Thakary stays with her
aunt for six months and has to attend a new school,
she is not at all pleased.

It's not long before she attracts attention from the school
bullies, but Sorin, a quiet Romanian boy, comes to the
rescue. Skye has no idea that Sorin has a secret of his own
– and his plans certainly don't include helping the
troubled teenage ghost who Skye has befriended.

A funny, moving new story from the author of
My So-Called Afterlife.